PARANOIA
(The Walk and Talk with Angela)

Caleb Kavon

Proverse Hong Kong

PARANOIA (The Walk and Talk with Angela) shows a man of solitary habits and a background of family disruption and multiple relationships. Disturbed by his girlfriend, Angela, who calls him "oblivious", he reflects on his past life, focusing on many people and topics that he previously ignored. He acknowledges his faults and selfishness, and finds cause to give thanks to all who have played any part in his life, including mother earth and the universe itself. It is through the *mea culpa* of his narrative that a picture emerges of his past empty and unhappy life. Gradually, this becomes intertwined with unusual events in his present life, meetings with new acquaintances and their stories, and a high-minded plot to expose and frustrate the alleged war-mongering plans of North Korea and end the screams of torture victims in "the camps".

For a long section of the text, this seems like a classic and detailed study of developing schizophrenia and paranoia, but the external plot proves that the strange present events experienced by the anti-hero have a real existence beyond his brain.

This, Caleb Kavon's third novella, bears his hallmark – reflective seriousness. His concern at the errors of individuals and the flaws in the societies they create and perpetuate is brightened by the suggestion that greater engagement and appreciation of what one has are first steps that we all could take.

CALEB KAVON was raised in Hong Kong and the Philippines. A former US army officer deployed in Central and South America, Kavon has lived and worked in China for the past seventeen years. He has travelled the world and remains an avid student of all things. Fluent in Chinese and Spanish, he currently lives in Chengdu, China and eagerly awaits the positive changes on our planet which he knows are possible.

ALSO BY CALEB KAVON
The Monkey in Me: Confusion, Love and Hope Under a Chinese Sky (Proverse, 2009)
The Monkey in Me; Chinese translation (Proverse, 2010)
The Reluctant Terrorist: In Search of the Jizo (Proverse, 2011)

PARANOIA
The Walk and Talk with Angela

Caleb Kavon

Proverse Hong Kong

Paranoia: The Walk and Talk with Angela
by Caleb Kavon.
Published in pbk in Hong Kong by Proverse Hong Kong January 2018.
Copyright © Proverse Hong Kong, January 2018.
ISBN: 978-988-8491-33-9.

1st pub. in pbk in Hong Kong by Proverse Hong Kong, 23 March 2012.
Copyright © Proverse Hong Kong, 23 March 2012.
ISBN 978-988-19934-7-2

Distribution and other enquiries to Proverse Hong Kong,
P.O. Box 259, Tung Chung Post Office,Tung Chung,
Lantau Island, New Territories, Hong Kong SAR.
E-mail: <proverse@netvigator.com>. Web: <proversepublishing.com>

Cover photograph by Courtenay Bickley.
Cover design by Artist Hong Kong Company.

Proverse Hong Kong

British Library Cataloguing in Publication Data (1st edition)

Kavon, Caleb.
 Paranoia.
 I. Title
 813.6-dc23

ISBN-13: 9789881993472

CONTENTS

ONE

PRELUDE

The day had started normally.

He had watched the news and eaten some toast.

Nothing unusual in the news, just some suicide bombings here and there.

Tensions in this place and that place, and a speech by some political leader.

Oh, yes and thousands of people were getting the flu.

He went out for his usual walk.

The first strange thing was a young man gripping a tightly rolled newspaper in his left hand. He was dressed completely in white. At first it seemed as if he was in some sort of medical gear, but when he looked more closely, he saw it was just an all-white track suit.

Further down the street, he saw a small girl riding a bright red bike. She was riding in circles with a very intense and serious gaze. As he passed she kept on making the same circle in the sidewalk, with the same tight diameter and the same number of pedal pushes, eight.

Next he saw an old lady and man walking down the street. The old lady was an albino completely white with pink skin, and the old man was carrying a plastic bag in one hand and a yellow umbrella in the other.

Further down the road, standing on the corner, was a young woman, with a green shirt and blue pants and matching blue tennis shoes. She had a lost look like she did not know where she should go next. She was not a beauty and a bit overweight. He wondered if she had lost her way or had a fight with her parents or her boyfriend or had been recently hurt by some cruel words. She was standing – but standing as if sitting – not moving, and the only sign of movement was the way the wind pushed the lower part of her curly hair gently to the left as the cool gusts past by. He almost wanted to talk to her, but she was not moving at all.

He turned down a streetroad and walked on. This was the same walk he did every day. After about twenty metres he realized that this was not where he turned every day. It must have been the girl or statue of a girl that he had just seen that had confused him. Anyway, he knew this street also, so no harm was done and he continued on.

You see all sorts of things when you walk in a city. In fact you can walk the same route every day and see something new. It was just that, today, he was seeing quite a few new and strange things.

The strange things did not end there.

He remembered the first time that he had returned home after a long absence and seen that his Father's hair had turned grey. He was sitting in a high-backed chair covered with the light from an oriental lamp. He had not known what to say. It was a bit shocking, that first sight of an older man. He looked the same and yet in a very serious way he was suddenly different. At the next corner, he saw a man who had the same profile as his father, he looked again and the man was gone.

In a nearby beauty parlor he saw another unusual sight. It was a woman who looked like his most recent ex-wife. But she looked like his wife had looked before he met her. She was the exact same person, and yet much younger. He knew this from some old photos he had seen. He tried very hard not to stare at her, looked one more time and kept walking.

"If that is a ghost, it is a pleasant one!" he thought out loud.

Then he remembered his goal of not talking that day.

"But talking to yourself should not count!" he answered himself out loud again.

Walking is a good time for thinking.

He remembered the night before with Angela. No, it was not a serious relationship. He met with her every month or two for some quick sex. She was married and so had he been when they met a very long time ago.

It was a strange and non-entangling relationship. They met whenever. Sometimes she called him. Sometimes he called her. Sometimes the schedule worked out, and sometimes it did not. Sometimes they ate at an Italian restaurant before the tryst. Sometimes they ate at an Indian curry house after the tryst. They had been doing this strange ritual for almost fifteen years now, or so he imagined.

Last night, she had looked at him in a very strange way, with an even stranger twinkle in her eyes, and started the following conversation, "You know, you seem to be seeing more all of the sudden."

"What do you mean, Angela?"

"Well you can be pretty oblivious you know."

"Oblivious?"

"Yes, like you are here, with me, and then you always seem to be somewhere else."

"Oblivious? We have been together like this for fifteen years."

"Well, it's just as I always thought. You never saw anything about me."

"Angela, I am not sure what you mean. We have had a kind of strange relationship; not sure how I was any more oblivious than anyone else."

"Its just like you were only there sometimes and now I feel like you are seeing things now. You know nothing is just about sex, don't you?"

He had looked at her and closely this time. She was not the young girl he had known. There were some wrinkles here and there and she now had the body of a middle-aged woman. The mascara on her face was streaked and there was a tear passing slowly down from the centre of her right eye.

It was true. He knew it immediately. He had never known her at all.

"Angela, thanks for telling me finally. I may have missed something here and there. Fifteen years is a long time for a couple to be together even in the way we have been together. Especially in the way we have been together. You have always been here for me, and truly I have not given it much thought. Let me try to focus more on what we have been together and what we had. Maybe I have missed a lot."

Angela then nodded and got dressed. She smiled again.

"Thanks for saying that. It means a lot to me."

A short kiss, another hopeful smile, and she was gone. No Indian food was on the schedule that night.

TWO

YOU WERE MY WORLD

You were my world. Not sure how I got here or why. This place was called Earth. I probably never figured out very much about you. It was just so easy not to think about you at all. Yes, in later years, we all thought about pollution or what we called global warming. Or, yes, I thought sometimes about this place or that place. Or I learned about our solar system. Or I saw pictures of this world shot from some passing space-craft. From space you seemed very blue.

I knew that you rotated on an axis and rotated around the sun. This world, you were my home for so long. Did I ever give you much thought, or do any of us? We are usually involved in our daily pursuits.

Me, particularly.

I am not sure I gave you more than one hour of thought in all my years. Maybe it was more. But in any case it was miniscule. After all, everything I breathed, ate or saw was a product of this planet and our life here.

I could see only the details. This place or that place. This thing or that thing. This situation or that situation of mine. You were everything to me and I never saw you and never gave you much time. I was captive to your days and nights and weather and seasons and I insulated myself away from you and missed it all. Without you, I would be nothing and there would be nothing.

You were my world and I knew you not. I was never even conscious that you existed in broader strokes than my poor eyes could see, or my spirit could perceive. Home to billions of people and trillions of thoughts and activities, I could see only what was in front of my nose at any one time. I could hear only my breathing and think only my thoughts while you provided me with everything for my time here. My blindness was incredible and my limitations were without limit. In your sight I am truly nothing and my small impact on you for so long is beyond humbling. My World, My World, My World, you were always there and I saw only myself every day of my life. My World! And I never realized how much more there was than me, myself and I.

How could I live with you for so long and miss it all? You were my life and I never even noticed; as if everything there is was all simply appropriate and my due.

Thank You and Sorry, I never even thought once about what it all meant. I lived with you and took and gave so very little back.

THREE

KALI AT THE GHAT

The Walk continued. He passed a store selling Indian things, like clothes and small statues. He thought he saw a small statue of Kali and he remembered....

A long time ago he had been in India. Somewhere in West Bengal but not Calcutta or Kolkata as it is called now. He remembered when they changed the name of Bombay to Mumbai, but the Kolkata name change he missed along with the change of the name of Madras to Chennai. He should probably have kept up with that one. Peking to Beijing was old hat along with Canton to Guangzhou. But the Kolkata name change kept him in the dark for a long time. He had probably gone five years or so before Chennai and Kolkata came into his viewfinder. Sometimes he would be at an airport and see a flight to Kolkata listed, and it never dawned on him that the flight was to Calcutta. The same with Chennai. How could they change the names and he never knew? That was a big knowledge gap. Or he was just stupid or ill-informed, or both. It still bothered him.

He remembered he had been in a market alongside some river, walking with his girlfriend at the time. He was enjoying it all, the shops, the smell of spices. Walking through the cool of the alleys and looking into the stalls was fun for the day and added some kind of adventure.

India is great if you are looking for strange things; and since people in India have some different beliefs and many gods, they are great to stare at, as you can look at them strangely and they will always reply in kind. Strange is good sometimes.

They had stumbled upon a small Kali Temple. In those days, tourists liked to walk around with big cameras; it was part of the tourist uniform. You wanted to take pictures of those interesting sights and things like that. Then you could blow them up and put them in your house or apartment as remembrances or put them in photo albums that somehow recorded your life. You wanted to take as many interesting pictures as you could. You probably spent more time taking pictures than you did seeing anything. But that was OK. It was just what you did when you went to a new place.

This Kali temple was very small. There was a small statue of her in the back of a small room and he remembered several men. One of the men was bald. He asked if he could take a picture of that Kali and the bald man said OK. The way he remembered it after all these years was that the bald guy was without teeth and he swore that there was blood on the bottom of the Kali statue.

He kept that picture in a small plastic frame for many years. In fact he thought he might still have it somewhere if he could find the time to look for it. At one time he fancied himself as a Kali devotee. She was so Indiana Jones. She had the power of death, the other side of the coin of life. She could back people up, and claim the eventual win. Heck, she could even try to eat her husband Shiva. She was all rage with a bracelet of skulls across her neck. Really that Kali was quite a show.

Later he became more enamored with Ganesha. Ganesha was kind of common sense. He, with his elephant head, could just kind of sit there smiling, and without jumping up and down have the universe move in its divine order. Ganesha was easier to follow, and besides, Ganesha would help you overcome obstacles, which he had always found very necessary in a daily sort of way. Ganesha was the God of Wealth and could manifest what was not manifested. He had four arms and all sorts of weapons and he was tough. He had fought his father, Shiva, to a stand-still as a child, and that was really quite an accomplishment, especially since he had done it all to defend his mother Parvati, the daughter of Brahma himself. And above all, he enjoyed just letting Ganesha run the show. You did not have to push too hard if you let him just handle your day. The funny thing was that Ganesha never failed. That was something you could count on unlike the names of certain very well-known Indian cities.

What he most remembered about the visit to the Kali temple is what he did not remember. What was his girlfriend saying that day? What did she think about it all? She was only a very, very small part of his memory, when she should have been a central character in it all. After all, he had said that he loved her. But looking back, he could hardly remember that she had even been there.

It was really that bad. He had been traveling with her for several months and it was now as if she had never been there at all. He could remember only what he had done and what he had been thinking at the time and what he had seen. All he had left at all from the trip was that one picture of Kali, which he had kept religiously for a very long time. The memory of his time with her was almost completely gone and forgotten, yet at the time she had meant everything to him.

He almost felt sick at the realization. Someone so close to him for so long and all he had left was a photograph of Kali to show for it. They had lost touch and she had fallen into the netherland of people lost in his life. That day was firmly in his mind, and she had disappeared somehow.

Angela was right. He had been missing a lot and for a very long time. There were not even words to express all that he had missed. That girlfriend should have been more to him than that picture of Kali.

He might be able to find the picture somewhere in his boxes of things, but could he ever get her back?

FOUR

YOU WERE SOMEONE I KNEW AND LOVED: ONE

I would really like to figure this one out. Yes I made a total mess of this relationship all by myself. Do the words, desertion, unfaithfulness, foolishness and immaturity mean anything at all to me? I left you for another woman and I made up a very good excuse. None of this was your fault at all. I made you suffer and there was no reason for it.

We had a life together. We had furniture and things and even savings. I broke that up all by myself and sadly it was not the first time. I talked a good show and let it crash. Yes, well, that has always been me. Talking a good show and letting it crash.

What happened to those two young people victimized by my stupidity? I made you cry for a long time and yet you somehow found the strength to carry on. Somehow you never blamed me for the complete error of my ways as if you had somehow done something wrong. Then you even had the grace to see and remember some good things that came out of it.

But I was a total jerk to you and for no reason at all.

But just to let you know, the u-turn that I made – or the quick short-cut I thought I was making – was just a path to a harder life. I chose my poison and yes, it has poisoned me and everything that I see. I find it hard to find any justification for my mistake and deserve any punishment I receive in this life or eternity. I was wrong in every way.

What did I do to you and the bright happy woman you should have been? Were we both stupid? Maybe. But there was no excuse for how I betrayed you. I recognized my error a long, long time ago. There was never a good excuse. I have lived as much less of a man and person because of the mistake I made with you.

How could I miss everything for so many years? It is only now that I am seeing what I did, and only now that slowly the memories come back of sunny days and an ordered life.

I will never completely understand why I threw it all away. I have lost so much because of this and I am glad that your life has been something, despite the crushing unjustified mistake that I made against you, your sanity and all that you deserved as a person. My head is bowed in humility and shame every time I think about you and my incredible and complete error.

Thank you, thank you for forgiving me., It was all my fault.

FIVE

SOCCER AND A MISSILE LAUNCH

He was still walking.

Several weeks ago, he had a meeting with a North Korean defector. Kim Kun was his name and he was dressed in black. He had been doing some freelance work and a friend recommended he meet a real defector to learn more about North Korea.

Now, meeting with defectors is a strange thing. I mean, what if they are not real defectors, but actually spies, or a fake defector or a double agent? Maybe they could be working for the New KGB or the infinitely capable CIA, or trading in weapons. You really can't be too careful in these kinds of situation.

Thus, he decided to meet this Kim Kun, or whatever his real name was, at a hotel bar near the Incheon International Airport. He knew the stale hygienic airport bar would be a fine and boring meeting place and probably safe. He would probably not be kidnapped in any case. But then again, the North Koreans only kidnap Japanese or movie stars or maybe soccer players. They probably would have no use for him. Anyway, better to be on the safe side.

Kim was waiting for him at the bar looking very neat. All in black with a V-necked black sweater and a gold watch and shiny patent leather shoes with of course very black socks. It all seemed very sinister.

He shook hands with Mr Kim. It was a firm grip and possibly the kind of grip which could result in a devastating tae kwon do flip or 007 smash to the neck. But nothing happened and they sat down.

The conversation started like this.

"Mr Kim, How long have you been in South Korea?"

"Oh, about eight years now."

"What do you think about the new South Korean culture?"

"Well, they like to dance."

"Oh."

Just then as if an angel came into the room, the Hotel Bar TV came on. Lo and behold, it was a FIFA World Cup qualifying game. And of course, it was South Korea versus North Korea.

Well, we all know how soccer crazy the South Koreans became during their World Cup. In fact it was a bit irritating to everyone else in the world. Yes, congratulations on hosting the World Cup, and congratulations on your team doing well in that very same World Cup. But please do not overdo it. Because of the emotive outpouring of national pride and the scenes of hundreds of thousands of South Korean fans taking to the streets, it was just uncomfortable.

They should make a rule that if you host the World Cup your team cannot participate, or for God's sake, should be eliminated in the first round. It just makes all the other fans nervous. You are out-numbered by the locals and really cannot root against them. You need at least partially to support them. You can't just root against them. But in your heart you want them to lose. The same for Germany, or Brazil, or Italy, or any team. Tell me the French beat Brazil three goals to none and I will sell you a one-way ticket to Somalia, tourist-class. The fix was in. Maybe others see it differently, but that World Cup made him hate the South Korean team forever; the French team too. They just over-did it.

So here he was in the boring hotel bar, which suddenly was not boring because of the soccer game, sitting with a North Korean defector. The South Koreans were all transfixed by the game and the North Korean was watching also.

This was going to be a key test. Which team would Mr Kim, the defector, support? If he supported the North, did it mean he was not a real defector? Or if he supported the South, had he sold out everything in his past? Or if he supported the South, was he really in heart supporting the North? Or even, should he dare to ask, since they were all Koreans anyway, why would they root for one team or the other? Funny how simplicity is very profound.

The game became very interesting. After several Jack Daniels and cokes, he was the only one who made a sound when the North Koreans attacked the goal; which made everyone in the bar look at him. Mr Kim did not show any emotion, but he did smile a lot.

One big secret about Asia is – when you are doing business in China – if they are smiling, they are killing you. If the Koreans are smiling, they are nervous. Mr Kim was smiling the whole game.

The game ended with the South Koreans winning One to Nil. The happy South Koreans made quite a show. Mr Kim was just smiling.

"Mr Kim, what did you think of the game?"

"I think that the North will soon fire a missile."

He said it very softly.

"Wow, that would be quite a reaction."

"Yes, that is the only response because of this game."

"A very serious response."

"Yes, it is all very serious to us. You might not understand."

"Actually, Mr Kim, I agree with you. I have never seen such a ridiculous situation. Two countries exist because no-one has the guts to challenge a dictator. We talk about suffering and democracy everywhere else but just let the Korean problem fester. It is a farce. Koreans have been treated terribly. I have met Koreans in Russia, in Uzbekistan and Kazakhstan and it is always a sad story. We really have been incredibly stupid and cruel to allow this ridiculous situation to carry on for so long. The United States, China, Japan and Russia are equally guilty in this travesty."

"Yes, that is why all the South Koreans can do is dance. Nothing else makes sense to any of us. Thanks for understanding and I hope both teams make it to the World Cup."

"Me too. as long as the World Cup is not here. You all drove me crazy last time."

"Oh."

Well he did not learn much about South Korea or North Korea from Mr Kim, but at least he got the World Cup issue off his chest. He thought just maybe Mr Kim was a real defector. And yes, the North did fire a missile several days later.

SIX

YOU WERE MY TEACHERS

Really something needs to be said here. If I live to be eighty – just a number; I probably won't make it that far – it means I will have spent roughly twenty-five percent of my life in school with you, my teachers.

I really can't remember most of your names. I was really like most people, I put effort into what I liked and ignored the rest. Not a sparkling repertoire, in any case. Did I ever show brilliance? No. Did I ever really appreciate you? No. I just kind of wondered what we were doing together anyway. Did you teach me anything I did not want to learn? Never.

Quite an odd relationship for one quarter of my life.

Yes, I remember some of your lectures. Yes, I remember the schools and some of you. In fact I did, during one of my mid-life crises, call several of you. But we went worlds apart. Did I ever get past that? Tto think of you as struggling humans, like I thought of myself? Probably not. But that is not my strength anyway. So much time in school, I missed it all, also.

Your ideas never became my ideas. Did you teach me to think? Probably not. I am still learning to do that. Isn't it a process we all go through? Since I can't point a finger at one really, really formative learning experience, does that mean I never learned anything? No. But it does mean that one quarter of my life was lost, since I never valued school in the way I should have. I was just too busy rushing to the next thing, place, stage, event or disaster in my life.

In fact, I almost have pity on anyone who had to teach someone as totally clueless as me. I am sure some of you figured it out. Like the one time I told my Algebra teacher that it was "my prerogative" if I was to study or not to study for the exam. Maybe I am being too hard on myself, and perhaps many of us are exactly the same. But that does not justify it in the slightest. When you miss twenty-five per cent of your existence in spite of the efforts of your teachers, you should be embarrassed, to say the least. I missed the spirit of school and it was a spoiled and stupid way to be. I wasted some of your time in this world for nothing. Of this I am very ashamed. I wish I could go back and really hear what you were saying, now that I am older.

Thank you. You tried to teach me. I just was not receptive enough to see what you had to teach me at the time.

SEVEN

RICHARD SORGE ON FIGHT-STREET

He was still walking.

But today, this street was fight-street.

Near the first building on the street he could hear a loud fight, the male-with-female kind. In this fight, the male was obviously winning. You could hear his loud insults flying, with just a small response from the female contestant. He could not see the fighters, but something was being broken, maybe a plate or picture or glass, or something like that.

Half a block down, a young couple was arguing in the street. In this match, the female was doing all the talking. Something about money, something about gambling, something about, "Where is the rent money?" and, "Why are you so irresponsible?" and, "How will we buy food?" and, "Why can't you ever keep a job?" He heard all this in just a few steps, and tried desperately not to look at the couple in the battle of wills.

Finally he got to his coffee-shop. Entering, he went to his favourite table. Here, he did not have to say a word. Thank God. They knew exactly what coffee he wanted, and just placed it in front of him. He had made it clear that he did not like to talk and just wanted his coffee. Actually in the past he did communicate with people; but just about two months ago he decided to go silent. Well, he did talk to some people; but not many; and never to anyone he had not known before.

It was just for the simple reason that he was in fact tired of hearing his own voice. So many years of such nonsensical talking had made his ears hurt at his own sound. He really pitied birds and other animals that needed to make noises constantly. He much preferred the life of a deer or an elk. They make noises only when it is time to mate. Sounded like a good match anyway and entirely logical. Good for the deer species! Silence was golden.

Of course, it was fight-street. And even in the restaurant a couple was arguing. This was one of those "time-to-break-up" arguments. The girl was telling the guy to get lost. At first she tried to be nice about it, but the guy was being crushed like an empty soda can by every word. You could see him slumping, see his love being crushed and his ego shattered.

So far the score was, Women: Two, and Men: One. Fight-street was alive. He looked around for the nasty and malicious spirit which was causing all this fighting this morning. He even looked himself over. Perhaps he was causing it all by his change in route, caused by the statue of the heavy-set girl on the street. Or maybe she was causing it all.

There are all sorts of inter-sex fights. Couples in love or out of love are the great event for so many. There is the post-drunken-night fight. There is the jealousy fight. There is the financial fight. There is the "just-in-a-bad-mood fight." There is the "lack-of-attention fight." There are so many, it is hard to keep up with them.

A complete life will include most of them. You need to experience them all, so that later you cannot say you missed one. Kind of like going on scary rides at an amusement park, or firing an automatic weapon, or watching every horror movie you can. Not to be missed.

But these fights are infinitely better when you are a participant. Hearing other couples fight is really not that great. The air is full of hate and misunderstanding. You cannot even escape it, you just hope that God will be kind and keep you out of it. Listening is hard enough.

The break-up fight was getting pretty ridiculous and it would go on for a while, as the man was trying almost to beg the woman to keep him on. He kind of wished him luck. Everyone deserves a break, especially the stupid men of the planet.

Yes fighting was part of life and love. And, come to think about it, he had had his share of fighting. Sometimes he won and sometimes he lost. But these were not his fights. And yet they were. He had heard almost each and every word in three fights in the last ten minutes, he guessed. Well, we cannot really avoid these things. And it was more interesting than watching TV. It was after all reality and not Reality TV. So he decided just to go ahead and suffer through it.

Another strange thing.

The table he always sat at had four seats. He always sat at the seat with his back to the far wall so he could look out of the window. In the seat to his right there was a book. He picked it up. It was a biography of Richard Sorge, the famous Soviet spy in World War II, who had informed Stalin with exactitude of the date of the Nazi invasion of Russia, 22 June 1941. Stalin had ignored him – either on purpose or out of distrust – and the rest was history. Sorge had been hanged by the Japanese on 7 November 1944 for espionage.

Unfortunately, he had to ask Manuel the waiter about it, which meant talking.

"Manuel, why is this book here? Whose is it?"

"Not sure, Sir. Never saw it before. You can have it if you want it. No-one was in your seat yesterday, that I remember. Not sure how that book got there."

"Oh."

A tough dilemma! He could read about Richard Sorge for a little while, or listen to a couple in the last throes of a nasty break-up. He had to think about this.

He looked at the inside of the book, and of course, there was Korean writing. Now that made sense. – Defectors and Korean books about Richard Sorge! – It almost sounded mysterious and nonsensical, except that it was just strange. All thoughts about it were nonsensical, like the pleas of the young man about to be executed by "Mata Hari", the love of his life.

Easy choice. When in doubt always go with Richard Sorge.

He flipped to the end. There was a picture of a Soviet postage-stamp with Sorge's face on it. Apparently Kruschev had made Sorge a hero almost twenty years later, after he heard the story from some Eeuropean movie about him.

The guy was very smart. Heck, there were a lot of smart people back then. There was Einstein, Oppenheimer, Sorge, Mao Tse Tung, Eisenhower, Ho Chi Minh, Chou En Lai, Churchill, Stalin, Kenyatta, Mahatma Gandhi, Somerset Maugham, Patton, Chuikov, Nehru, Sakarno – or was that Sukarno? What had happened since then?

Sorge apparently had had a Japanese lover, who had visited his grave outside Tokyo every day until she died in 1970. Always a bit of romance in these spy-stories; and Sorge was a lucky guy.

At least he wasn't getting dropped like the poor guy over there in the long-lost-before-it-began struggle to get his girlfriend back.

But getting hanged is no picnic either. Forget the postage stamp, Comrade Krushchev!

He took the book away from fight-street and the coffee-shop. Back to his castle.

The girl was still just standing there. Now she was looking at her cell-phone.

EIGHT

YOU WERE ALL THE PEOPLE I NEVER KNEW

Yes, this list is pretty long. You are probably the lucky ones. I saw you everywhere, in your cars, at the airports. Or I saw the lights of your apartments lit warmly at night in yellow. Sometimes you sat next to me on the plane and we never spoke. You were in other classes than meI. You lived down the road or on the other side of the planet. There were billions of you.

In fact, I probably met only several thousands of all the inhabitants of this planet. I had nothing to do with most of you. I would see you on the street sometimes and even look at you, but we never met – billions of you, whom I never knew.

Your situation is the same as mine. You were as stuck as I was stuck, by knowing only those that you knew. What a situation; to live without the ideal friend or perfect mate or worst enemy that you never met. We just couldn't avoid it, it would be impossible to know everyone.

Just a fact of life.

Probably your lives and happiness and frustrations were not that different from mine. We all started the same, being born; and we will all end the same in death. Are the details and differences really that important? Was my life more interesting, or was yours? Do we want to be like Bill Clinton, or are we happy being ourselves? Or do we want to be like Hillary Clinton instead?

For sure, we have all had problems. Equally for sure, we were glad for each day that had fewer problems. For some of us life has been horrible, a life of war and death. For others it has been cruise-ships and golf-courses. Not sure why.

How could I know? I never got to know most of you, and I was usually too interested in my own little situation to think of yours. And you were probably too interested in your own situation too, to care about mine.

This is really one of the great pities of life. We focus only on ourselves. And this is true of all of us. Yet we share so much here on the planet. The sun, moon and air and our little area, whether it is desert, mountains or valleys. And we share it only with those we know.

Not really logical.

Anyway, this is just to let you know that I finally figured out that you were here with me. I wish all of you the best and hope I did as little damage as I could to you. At the same time, I am not satisfied with what I did do.

Thank you for being here with me. Sorry we never met. You might have helped me, and maybe – just maybe – I might have helped you. But judging from my record here on Earth, that is a very small maybe.

NINE

AN EMAIL FROM A TEACHER

Arriving to the solace and silence of his small rented room, and the mess from last night's cigarettes, it was time to work. The project had to be completed, but of course not today. A great pleasure in life is when you can say, "Why not tomorrow? The world is not going to fall if I don't get it done today." Yes that was the answer. Not today. Maybe just a peck here and there. Then mayy be he will actually work. Just let the day occur as it will.

Well it did occur. The first event was an email from the teacher of one of his children. Apparently, his son had told the teacher to go to hell the day before.

Time for parenting was called for. The great balancing act was in play. The sins of the father.

There was just time to call his child at the home of the ex-wife, before the night fell in another continent. God bless time-zones.

"Christian, what happened at school?"

"Nothing, Dad. I am getting sick of this teacher. He is driving me crazy."

"You know you can't do that. I want you to write a letter of apology to the teacher immediately and give it to him tomorrow. Really. This is just ridiculous. So many people losing their homes, people without food. And you have time for stupid fighting with your teachers. Do you understand? I am having a hard time financially and you make me deal with crap like this. Do you understand?"

"Yes, Dad, I do. I am just sick of him."

"Well, Christian, wait until you are my age and you will have so much more to be sick of. Just do the work and see what happens. They are trying also to teach you. No more of this, please!"

"OK, Dad."

"OK, now this has ruined my morning. Go to bed now and get your act together. You know I am trying to go silent and then you make me talk about insane things like this."

"OK, Dad."

"And I love you."

"I love you too."

So that was parenting. He had done what he had to do. He had played the "I-am-your-father" role. He had done it before and would do it again. God, he loved his children, and God, he hated to see himself in them. They seemed to get all his bad points. And the good points, whatever they were, were lost. What good points, anyway?

Of course, no-one thinks these things through before you have children. You never see the day fifteen years later when you will be having a "fatherly" conversation with the children. Actually, God was kind. Parenting gets easier with time and the more children you have. Each one teaches you more about yourself, and each problem seems smaller as you see it again.

Children teach us more about ourselves than they ever learn from you. They give, you receive. They love you and you worry. They get older and you age beyond recognition. They bound into life as you did once, and you bounce down a rocky hill of exasperation and confusion. They are blessed by youth and you are cursed by experience. They are optimistic and you are cynical. You know they are right about so much but you just cannot say it. You need to see them into the future safely.

You really cannot fail unless you try. Your children are something you can really get results out of. They want you there. If you are there for them, you will succeed. If you see yourself and your failures in them, you will do a good job. You will love them, you just cannot help it.

Absence does make the heart grow fonder. He was a better parent because he was not there always. But who is? Your children do their things in the day, you do yours. You see them late at night and early in the morning. It is almost better to have a bit of separation. It is like church used to be on Sunday. Once a week; a good counsel. And you are set for the next stretch of life.

Well, that made his day. He felt needed and loved. God bless his kids – all of them. They were worth all the suffering, and they always gave you more than you received.

Back to silence. Back to not talking. Back to another day.

Yes, nothing goes as planned. But it is these changes in plans that make our life interesting. He guessed he could say a couple more words than he wanted to say, if it was for a good cause.

TEN

YOU WERE MY CHILDREN

Sweet angels. The blessings of my life. One thing that was not a complete failure. My greatest burden, that was simply my greatest joy.

I never thought I could do anything well at all. You made it so easy for me. I loved how we worked through life's problems. I loved how you could forgive me for my mistakes with an, "Oh, that's just how Dad is." I loved how you accepted me as I was. I loved how I did not have to be a star, for you to love me. I loved how we laughed and joked, and how you could always make fun of me and I enjoyed it.

You made everything right.

We did not have a perfect family, no-one does. But you made the best of it. I somehow managed to support you, but not perfectly. Maybe we should have had more vacations, or more time together in what is rapidly an ending time.

I think you knew me. I was as open with you as I could have been. Well, then again, I was as open about everything as I could have been. It's like what we talked about one time. Your greatest weakness is sometimes your greatest strength, and your greatest strength is sometimes your greatest weakness. It just depends on the situation.

Yes, I know I was boring. I liked to read books, not go to the mall to shop. I never let you do anything dangerous, because I could not bear the thought that anything could ever happen to you. I missed so many days of your life. You did not miss too much with me. I was not that interesting. You were fascinating to watch. I was not.

I had to play a role with you. But that is how it is. As parents we need to take care of you; that is our first instinct. Even if sometimes I had problems with your mother, at least you knew we loved you. And that was not a failure.

You know I just want you to have good, happy, safe lives. I hope you learned something from me, I learned a lot about myself by being with you. You are all beautiful, different and special. I pray that you always do better than I did, which is not a big challenge.

But our times will be different; and – with the way the world is going – I am worried. But we will cross those bridges when we come to them. And we will cross those bridges as a family.

You know that my most cherished dream is that you will always stay together after I am gone. I hope you stay close to each other; that is what family is about, and you can do it.

I hope I said most of what I needed to tell you about life. I do really want to go silent soon or at least as silent as I can.

Thank you. You were everything that was good to me. Funny how what I thought was the toughest job in life ended out to be the best thing I ever did. I love you.

ELEVEN

WHEN A FRIEND OPENS UP – PIRATES MORE RICHARD SORGE

For some reason, he thought about a conversation he had had with a friend, Carlos, several weeks before. It was fascinating really, not for the friendship itself but for how much he had missed. Again.

He had known Carlos for a few years. Carlos came to visit him in China for about two weeks every year. And incredibly he had never noticed anything about him at all. Carlos was very intelligent, but in a kind of off-hand way. He had a way of getting his way without even letting you see what he was doing. He would play the fool and let people tease him, and just responded with a kind of small soft laugh.

You could tell that Carlos was honest, or at least more honest than most. Or was it, rather a sense of honour that he exuded? He liked to be on time and get things done. Everyday had an objective. When it was time to work, that is what he did. Carlos would make recommendations which made good sense, and of course these were missed.

Sometimes he would make the same recommendations every year. And yes, always the recommendations were missed.

During the last trip, he had decided to do things Carlos's way this time. He was going to try to be silent and just listen to him. What had been a burden in the past would be OK this time. He really had not done a good job with Carlos before and this time he decided to try just to listen. Anyway it fit in. He was sick of talking anyway.

Amazing. It worked. They had a better time than in the past. He let Carlos lead the way and found that he really enjoyed everything. Instead of forcing himself during the process, it worked better if someone else did the driving.

One day, after a long drinking session, Carlos opened up about a sad event in his past. Finally he felt comfortable enough to do so. He cried. You could finally see the person inside. What was really something was that Carlos had done really well in spite of this great challenge he had experienced in his youth. He had done an honourable thing and paid a price. When he could see this, he felt better.

All of this had happened because, for once, he had been silent. Talking and opinions just get in the way. He had missed Carlos the person because he had been so engrossed with himself for so long. Selfishness and self-interest blind us. How had he managed to miss Carlos for so many years? How had he missed everything? Why did he learn things so slowly in life? Everyone was there helping him all the time and he never even observed the most basic things. The regret of missing so much was mixed with this realization. But mostly it was just regret. Angela was right.

Then he thought again, for some reason, of pirates in the Gulf of Aden. The US Navy was chasing a dinghy with five Somali pirates who had kidnapped an American. That was the main news.

He picked up the Richard Sorge book with the Korean writing on the inside cover that had magically arrived at his table. Sorge had been severely injured, serving in the German Army in World War One. During his recuperation, he had become a communist through reading Marx and Engels and had participated in the wave of socialist-inspired strikes which had helped disrupt the Weimar Republic. After this he became a communist spy and was sent to China in 1930, acting as a German newspaper-correspondent, and even infiltrating the Nazi Party. There was a funny story about how he had stopped drinking, because he feared drinking would make him say too much at the beer-hall Fascist events that he attended.

It must have been interesting to become a fake Nazi. At the same time, you were working against them; and it probably took incredible self control. Lord knows how many beers he had to turn down. Those German beer parties get pretty crazy. Wine parties are different. People are more open to discussion. The world might have been different if there had been wine halls and not beer halls. But who really knows why what happened did happen anyway?

He decided to go downstairs and see if the girl was still standing on the far corner. Sure enough, she was there and still looking at her phone. Someone is having a breakdown. What do you do?

He would check on her later. She might be there for a while.

People fall and people rise. People get crushed and people survive. The poor girl was paralyzed on the street. What would he do? In a city of millions, what should you do?

The panorama of life is so fascinating. We have places to go. It is almost like being in a zoo. There is the young, confident animal. There is the old, frail animal. There is the animal about to be killed by the lion. More like the savannah than a zoo. More like the jungle than a zoo. Nature. We pass and watch and thank God that it is not us. We do not have the time to get involved; that is for someone else. We cheer the heroes and ignore the injured. We want to be in the group that makes it through the river, and we forget the ones that get stuck and do not survive. We put our infirm and aged in homes so that we do not have to see them, until it is us that are about to fall and then we wonder what the hell we were thinking about for all those years.

And we read stories about Soviet super-spies when we should really be doing something else; and call it a great day.

TWELVE

YOU WERE MY ENEMIES
(OR JUST NOT MY FRIENDS)
– ONE OR THE OTHER

You were the ones who did not like me, or even hated me. You were the ones I should have loved the most. We should love our enemies first. Support the prodigal son.

I have spent a lot of time thinking about you.

I am not sure why we did not get along. I really think it was usually my fault.

Maybe it was by my over-aggressive attitude or know-it-all approach. Maybe it was the short insult I gave you, or the way I did not seem to care what you thought. Maybe it was how I gave you the idea that I thought I was superior to you. It could have been one of a thousand things, I was hardly a saint, and if I were you I would not have liked me either. In fact, I am not amazed that you did not like me; I am more amazed by those who did like me.

I really almost preferred that you did not like me. I treated everyone – almost everyone – the same way. I was completely indifferent to what people thought of me. And if so many of you were turned off by me, well it only made sense.

Some of you just avoided me, and thought ill of me. That was most of you. You never said, one way or the other, and I just had to figure it out that you did not like me. Since I was slow at this, like at everything else, it probably took a long time.

Some of you made it very obvious, either by words or actions, but that was fewer of you.

In any case, I know I deserved it. I was oblivious. I was cruel. I was heartless. I only looked out for myself. I saw what you had – if it was more than what I had – and was jealous. If I had more than you, I made sure you saw it. If you were humble, I was arrogant. If you were arrogant, I was worse.

You know some people say, "Well you can't please everyone." That is true. You cannot go through life making everyone happy, that is impossible. But that is not the question. I never worried who I was pleasing or should please; and I know that for most of you, if I had somehow not been such a complete jerk, we would have gotten along fine.

This is a hit on me and not you. I was really usually the worst part of the situation. I was just that sort of person. No excuses made, and none intended. I could have had more friends, and fewer of you, if I had made the effort. I learned too late, and for many of you there are no good memories of me.

Maybe there are no memories at all, because we all try to forget those people, who – like me – are not good at treating people correctly. I would do the same.

You know, I do imagine perhaps I was innocent sometimes, and that some of you were wrong and later thought I was a better person than you first perceived. But – to be completely honest – I really need to say it was usually me at fault, the vast majority of the time.

Thank you. I am sorry things did not work out between us. I hope the impact of my cruelty did not last a long time. But I fear – with my bitter tongue and cruel words – for some of you it did. I am sorry, truly sorry. It was waste, all of it. My mistake.

THIRTEEN

CANDY AND DEATH

He checked his refrigerator. Empty. Now that would be OK, really it would be. But he had not eaten for several days, on purpose. His stomach was growling. Richard Sorge was getting boring, and he did not want to work at all.

Out to the store.

This would give him a chance to check on the statue girl, if she was still there.

Yes, she was.

And she was still staring at her cell-phone. Unmoving.

He walked up to her.

"Are you OK?"

No answer, no movement. Again.

"Are you OK?"

No answer, no movement. Again.

"Are you OK?"

This time a bit louder.

She moved only her eyes toward him.

"Are you OK?"

She spoke.

"Yes. No need to get involved."

"Actually, I don't want to get involved. But I was just wondering if you were OK. You have been here for a while. So I was just checking. And you are hardly moving."

"Yes. No need to get involved."

"OK. Just checking. I hope you are OK."

Her eyes went back down to her cell-phone. She went back to being a statue.

The walk to the store was short, about 350 steps, as he was counting. There is nothing wrong with counting your steps. There is no rule against it. Counting steps is OK because it keeps you from thinking about things like statues, like missed work, like other things. So it was fine.

The process of buying things was not fine. What do you buy? He got some instant mashed potatoes. That was good, he knew where the mashed potatoes section was, and mashed potatoes never hurt your teeth and are very filling.

Then he got a sport's drink. He would give this to the statue as an offering, if she was still there when he got back.

The candy section was a problem. There were over forty different types of chocolate. He was not against freedom of choice by any means. But at what point does too much choice exist? At what point does having forty types of chocolate and thirty types of ice-cream and thirty types of cookies become confusing? You cannot choose all of them and if you want to peruse the entire selection, your brain will become weak and you will spend an inordinate amount of time deciding. The same with TV-channels, models of cars, blankets, pillows, furniture and so many others. Yes, the market will decide. But what about our brains? Can they really choose between thirty different things without total confusion?

He gave up and chose one chocolate bar. Really it probably didn't matter. He also got some raisins, eggs, bread and some potato chips and made his way out of there after giving his money to the check-out person, who strangely enough resembled the statue girl.

The statue girl was still there. He put the drink next to her right foot and left.

Back to his castle.

He turned the TV back on. Then he turned it off. Then he turned it on. Then he turned it off.

It is really a battle. Silence versus noise. The TV is like another person. It talks to you. You cannot talk back. Philosophically, yes, you can be alone with the TV-set on. But you cannot be silent. You can turn the volume off and see the pictures. That is another option.

He turned the TV on, and turned off the volume. Good compromise.

If only there was a Japanese movie on, he could survive. But none appeared.

He looked out of the window. The statue girl was of course still there. Then he looked down and saw some leaves that had fallen on the window-sill from one of his many plants.

Leaves always fall. He did not know how long one leaf lasts. But they all fall down sooner or later. Even in hot climates, the leaves fall.

He had been at a Buddhist temple with one of his girlfriends recently. The temple had a very peaceful feeling and he liked to visit it on occasion. It was famous for the statues of 577 Arhats, or Enlightened Ones. These were really people like you and me, who had somehow attained enlightenment, and thus did not have to be reborn again.

They spent a long time visiting the statues. He really loved them. They all had different poses and expressions. The names were in Chinese, and he never knew the stories of their lives. There was probably a list somewhere. They were really a bit like saints. But instead of going to heaven, they had achieved heaven on earth and did not have to be reborn. Sounded like a reasonable trade.

Behind the temple was a crematorium. He had never seen it before. His girlfriend figured out where it was because there was a small cement smoke-stack coming out of the small building and at that time there was a family chanting Buddhist prayers and a couple of them were crying.

His girlfriend was quite spooked by it all and asked if the crematorium scared him at all.

He said no and pointed to some leaves on the ground.

"Look at the leaves, they all fall. Look at us humans, we all fall. Why be scared. Are the leaves afraid? This is all the Buddhists are saying. Look at everything. It all falls.

She looked at the leaves. "But if they were Christian leaves, they would fall and go to heaven."

"Yes, but what would the leaves do in a Five Star Hotel? Heaven is just a Five Star Hotel."

She looked back at the crematorium. "Well, I prefer the Five Star Hotel to this place. Let's go now so I do not have any more bad dreams. I always have bad dreams when I see a place like this.

"OK, let's go home. But it's not going to be heaven."

"I know that already. Life with you is not a Five Star Hotel. It's more like a crematorium. You always want to tell the truth. You really are too honest."

"Oh. I guess I will need to turn up the temperature for you some more."

She laughed, but the laugh was more of a frown.

FOURTEEN

YOU WERE MY COUNTRY

What an arbitrary thing, where I was born.

I could no more pick my country than my parents. You are born to one place or one race or one religion. You simply have no choice in this. Yet is completely defines you. You are that place. People define you by that place. If you are from a great and important country, you display that in all that you do.

Everyone has a country. Not really a special thing. We love to say, this country is like this, or that country is like that. But what are we saying? Why do we take pride in our country over others? Or why do we criticize our country as opposed to another? It is not like "they" in the other country were specially picked for birth there, no more than we were specially picked for birth in our country.

We spend an incredible amount of time on this kind of thinking, really an incredible amount of time. We watch one country rise or fall and then count gold medals in the Olympics. We say, that country is a mess and, this country is great. The whole country thing infects all of us.

If I had one US dollar (see country again) for each time I had to talk about my country I would be rich financially. But maybe I would be poor mentally. If that is all we have to talk about, so much of the time – and it is really not a special skill to be of one country or another – are we not wasting our time completely?

If you are scratching your head, so am I. I could go on and on about my country. And you could go on and on about your country. But is it really all that interesting?

Rather, I think it is more like the weather, which we also talk about endlessly and make comparisons about. The weather is really nice here and really bad there. Once again, we cannot control the weather or climate in one place, as opposed to another.

You were my country. I am not sure why.

But it sure is important and really makes a difference.

But it was not because I chose you.

I might even love you. I might even defend you, as others defend their countries and love their countries.

Thank you. You are me. I was blessed. But I am not sure why.

FIFTEEN

CONDOMS, KINGS AND EATING EGGS WHILE WATCHING COOKING SHOWS

One thing he liked to do was study the Chinese emperors. There were so many. He liked to memorize their names and what years they had ruled. Not that he knew much about them. But at least he knew their names and the dates. Learning about them could come later. Two thousand years of emperors was really quite a list. Anyway, it was something to do.

He had a friend coming in from Thailand soon. Thailand was the great expatriate fun place and playground and they had a great shopping arcade. He could not remember much about the airport, except one time he had seen a fantastic condom advertisement there.

The advertisement was really incredible. There was just this couple looking at each other. They were not ugly and not super-star-like handsome either. They were a bit normal really for an advertisement, not model types. What was fascinating was the photo itself. It just said everything.

The couple were looking at each other. The guy was smiling with a, "Well I am going to get lucky tonight look." The look was perfect, a smile with a sense of accomplishment. The girl's look was also right on. She was smiling in response; something like, "And I am going to give it you tonight, you lucky boy! Not sure that I really like you, but what the heck."

He had never seen a more telling picture. It was the best advertisement he had ever seen. It was better than the Mona Lisa or the Sistine Chapel, or a war on starvation photo. It said lust without the caution. It said, "Tonight is the night." Good advertisement, great advertisement, the best advertisement ever.

It was all he remembered of the Thai airport. But it was a good memory.

There was some sort of problem going on in Thailand at the time. There was the red team and the yellow team and each was appealing to the King of Thailand. One side was getting shot, and the other was wearing yellow and not getting shot. One side was from the provinces, and one side had all of Bangkok, or so it seemed.

41

There was Thaksin, who used to be a super-hero to the West, but not anymore. He owned a UK soccer team in blue uniforms and was the head of the red team. Then there was the Barbie Doll or Ken Doll, new Oxford-educated, non-elected, new, Prime Minister and he was the darling of the yellow team.

Anyway, you had to wonder what was going on. Could there ever be real change, and were the two sides going to go to the wall fighting? Really, it was confusing.

One side of him wanted them to just go for it. Get it over with. Fight it out. The other side was thinking, "No, they are not really going to do anything. They never do. It's all talk and always is in Thailand."

You get tired of nothing happening in south-east Asia. All the countries had been in a frozen state for so long. Myanamar, the Philippines, Malaysia, Indonesia and Thailand had been unchanging for so long. Singapore was another of the unmoving ones. Maybe they would be radical and devalue their currency. Vietnam and Cambodia were the same story. Nothing was happening.

He was sure the king would figure it out. Really he loved the King of Thailand. And he loved the Queen of England. He loved all the royalty really. The King of Belgium was great too. And let's not forget the King of Swaziland or the deposed Romanovs.

He loved all royalty. Why not?

Speaking of royalty, there was a regal, long-haired, pony-tail-wearing guy from Australia doing a cooking show on the TV. He was comparing eating a three course meal to sex. He was going on and on about how the flavours of this dish and that dish just explode in your mouth. It was maybe even better than sex, he opined as he poured the liquid from the intestines of a squid into the saucepan, which was crackling hot with garlic, butter, sugar, and who knows what else.

There were some shots of people stuffing food into their mouths inside his restaurant. You could see the lipstick on the lips of the female patrons smearing. It was indeed exhilarating. All that flavour was engrossing and gross at the same time. The cavemen probably were just as happy, ripping the meat off of a saber-toothed tiger.

He had been going to eat some eggs, but the cooking show kind of killed his focus. Eating eggs was kind of gross. They had no structure. Boiled, fried or baked or scrambled,it was always the same.

Soft on the teeth and basic in the mouth.

When he ate eggs there was no explosion of flavour. What did the Australian cooking king have that he did not have? Explosions of flavour just were not happening.

He put some eggs in the frying-pan and tried to imitate the chef. He cracked the eggs open with a flourish, and thought about the great flavour and exquisite ingredients in his eggs. He mixed the eggs with the same sense of purpose that the chef had displayed.

But it was not to be. He could not be the chef. Eating was not as good as sex.

In disgust, he threw the eggs away and sat down in total and unkind frustration. The cooking show had killed his desire to cook anything and eating eggs was not what he wanted to do anyway.

He thought of the condom advertisement one more time. Finally he concluded that he would rather wear a condom than eat eggs. The advertisement was just that good.

SIXTEEN

YOU WERE MY BROTHER

What was my problem? What evil inhabits my soul? What is my problem?

I only had one brother.

One.

Only one person came from the same womb as me.

One.

Only one person shared my flesh and blood.

One.

One person had the same parents.

One.

Yes.

One.

And it was crazy. It was as if I preferred everyone on Earth to you.

What is my problem?

I was terrible. I was a failure as a brother.

Yes, we never looked or acted the same way. I was loud and abrasive and you were somewhat quiet. I said anything I felt like saying and you thought before you spoke.

You did what you should have done in life. You listened and learned. I was a fool.

We went through the same mess that our parents left. We were together in the big storm, in the waves and earthquakes that should have been a home. It messed me up. I am sure it did the same to you.

Was I so confused that I never even saw you? Was I such a failure that I could not rise above my mistakes?

What sort of brother was I?

I know.

I teased you incessantly. I enjoyed your pain. Really, living with me must have been a sentence to hell. You must have been thankful for the day of liberation when I finally left the home and you did not have to suffer my torments any more.

Yes, we all have problems. Yes, you are not perfect. But why did we never have any brotherly feeling? We were that crippled. We were that different. We were cast off into the world of other people and places and never could have even what we could and should have had.

We feel like we never had a brother. We feel alone. We were not together. I never praised you as you deserved and we lived as if there was nothing there at all. We have both paid the price of being only children without brothers.

I am embarrassed beyond words.

I should have been close to you. But I was not there for you at all.

It was a failure.

It was a disaster.

What kind of human am I? I could not even get along with my brother.

I might as well have been born with one leg or one arm. I am disabled. I am a cripple. To miss the most obvious is not to live.

I had only one brother in this life. It was you.

I missed it all. I missed your life. All of it.

I was so blind.

I am so sorry.

Thank you. I have some memories. I should have so many, that I cannot pick what to remember of you. There should have been so much more.

I love you. Can't say I always did. But I always will. Brother.

SEVENTEEN

EARTHQUAKES, EAR PLUGS AND EATING ICE
WHY WE DRINK

He quickly turned off the cooking-show.

He got a glass and filled it with ice.

This was his lunch.

Eating ice. It was filling and it also cooled down your fever. Better than eggs.

Besides it is just water. It lasts longer. It is colder. You can eat it.

On the airplanes, they give you some ice and some liquid in a cup. The ice displaces the liquid. You drink it and all that is left is ice.

Besides they say the ice is melting on the polar ice-caps.

So ice really is an important and rare thing after all.

He put his earplugs in.

This was a new thing. He had started wearing earplugs. During the last Chinese New Year it had gotten so loud that he had put paper in his ears.

He liked it.

You could still hear, but you missed much of the other noises. You did not hear everything as loudly. You missed some irritating noises like cars and buses. You could not hear the planes flying overhead as loudly. When people talked to you, you could hear them, but not as much. And when you talked, they could hear you.

And you could hear yourself breathe and think. And you slept better.

The ears never close. They are always alert. They always are hearing.

In fact, you might be able to listen better if you heard less.

Really he thought everything had gotten too loud. There was so much noise and most of it was irritating. What sounds were so great?

Cars? No.

Buses? No.

Planes? No.

People talking loudly in restaurants? No.

People arguing? No.

People getting drunk? No.

Loud music. No.

Cell-phones going off? No.

People answering cell-phones? No.

Flushing the toilet? No.

Doors closing and opening? No.

Endless talking on television or radio? No.

Well, he did like the sound of the ocean, and the music of the erhu – that wailing, sad, Chinese instrument. He also liked Tibetan chanting. Bird calls and whale sounds could be OK. And he liked the sound of the wind in the trees.

But there werewas not that many good sounds when you considered all the other sounds that you did not want to hear; or that were just too much for your ears.

There was just too much noise. Earplugs were the answer.

He just knew that this was the future. More and more people would be wearing them and more and more people would find them comfortable. They really helped calm you down.

There was just too much noise.

Then again, sometimes there is not enough noise.

He had gone to Sichuan to help with the recent earthquake.

Now, there he had seen silence, so much silence.

There was the silence of destroyed houses, with all the people inside dead. There was the silence that came from the screams of the parents of lost children and family members. It could be loud outside, with ambulances and yelling as people sifted through the rubble. But there was real silence in knowing that the dead could hear no more.

Then there was the silence of the young soldiers helping with rubble when their officer came up driving a BMW to "inspect" the work for one hour before lunch, and promptly left. That is another kind of silence. He was not sure what type of silence it was.

Just a look silence.

Just hate and disregard silence.

Just all that we lose all the time silence.

Anyway it was a silence there in the earthquake zone.

But that is not the kind of silence you want to find. Earplugs are better. Use them first.

It had started to rain. Steady not hard, or was it hard not steady? It was raining and it was cold outside.

He looked outside. He had to check on her. Was she still there?

Yes, the statue was still there.

Poor statue.

Of all the statues in the city, she was the most vulnerable today. And not a landmark by any means, she was more in the category of an eyesore. Crushed and desolate. She was screaming for help so loud. She was screaming so loud and had broken the sound-barrier and become invisible to all the passers-by. That was why no-one seemed to be able to see her or hear her screams.

He went outside and put a blanket over her shoulders and left an umbrella by her side. Even statues can suffer in the rain.

But, other than that, he did not get involved.

It was really not surprising why people drank alcohol, or smoked hashish, or abused drugs, or became statues on a lonely city street. We could pretend all we wanted that they had problems and we had none. No, we all had problems. The statue had hers and he had his.

It was simple to see. We all had problems and that was that.

I am, therefore I have problems.

I am, therefore, I drink.

I am, therefore I smoke

I am, therefore I age.

I am, therefore I learn slowly.

I am, therefore I am like everyone else.

I am, therefore I want more than I have.

I am, therefore I see your faults.

I am, therefore you see my faults.

I am, therefore I hurt.

I am, therefore I hurt others.

I am, therefore I make mistakes.

I am, therefore life crushes us all.

I am, therefore ashes to ashes.

I am, therefore I need.

I am, therefore I bleed.

I am, therefore I try to love.

I am, therefore I sometimes lose at love.

I am, therefore I want.

I am, therefore I forget.
I am, therefore I want to forget.
I am, therefore I fail.
I am, therefore I fall.
I am, therefore I die.
We can pretend all we want. We can wear earplugs and eat ice. We can go to earthquakes and feel the silence of the dead. We can stand for hours looking at our cell-phone in the rain. We can lose everything. We can buy thirty types of ice-cream and shop till we drop.
We all have problems, especially statues in the rain.
It is just that simple.

EIGHTEEN

YOU WERE MY LIFE-STYLE

Oh, wasn't I something with my sunglasses and cologne! Fifteen suits adorned my closet. I always had more than I needed.

When I got a new car, it was not long until I started to think about my next new car. When I got a new house, I was already looking at my next new house. When I went to buy socks in the store, I made sure I bought ten pairs of socks and not one. When I bought shirts, I bought six instead of one.

I had it all. Cable TV and air-conditioning, I had to have them.

I kept up with the styles. That way I could buy even more.

I needed to keep up, you see. I could not fall behind. The more I had, the more I wanted. It was never about what I needed, it was about getting more of what I wanted.

It was just expected that I should have all this. It was just expected that I use my credit-card to buy what I thought I should have. Thrift, savings and sharing were not in my vocabulary. I could not understand those who saved and I could not understand that I ought not to have more than I needed.

When I drank, I drank more in one night than a sane person would drink in one month. When I smoked it was three packs. When I womanized, I had a great eye. I had to over-do it all.

I lived with more and more and considered it normal.

It was empty. It was vain. It was foolish. It was inconsiderate. My lifestyle gave me no happiness or meaning. I did not need all that I had been given for so long. I never appreciated anything anyway. I could just not be content with what I needed. I had to accumulate for the sake of accumulation. I had more junk and garbage than most on the world have to use.

When someone would point out my wasteful ways or just smile at my stupidity, I would become angry, and my selfishness would just shine through even more clearly. It was impossible that I should live with less. I somehow deserved it, I thought.

I could never wake up to the fact that I lived in excess. I could never wake up to the fact that sometimes less is more. I could never believe in simplicity. I was completely missing it all, again and again.

I was not the only one. But I was wrong. I was wrong. I was wrong every day and in every manner possible. I did not deserve anything. I only abused myself and others. To live in excess, with more than you need, is nothing more than stupidity. Having more than you need is the life of a fool.

Thank you, life-style. My blessings were too many. I did not appreciate even one.

NINETEEN

BRUCE LEE – ELVIS – MISSION ACCOMPLISHED

He tried to think about some of his heroes.

Well, there were just two.

Bruce Lee and Elvis.

He was convinced that the world ended as soon as they died. He was convinced that everything had gone down-hill from the moment they were gone. He was convinced that nothing good had happened since they left the world.

Why?

It was just that simple. They were super-heroes. They were not human. They were beyond all of us.

Bruce Lee. Who had better kung fu than him? Who was in better shape? Who made better movies?

When he was a child, all he hoped for was to be like Bruce Lee. He was everything. His style of kung fu was the best. He was not doing shampoo commercials. He was not interested in the world. He was above all of us. He just wanted peace and quiet. He was happy with his family. He was modest and humble. He did not have to show off. He was wearing the most recent fashions. He had learned something from the world. He never said stupid things.

There would never be anyone like him. We might move on to other heroes and have different lives and desires. But there was only one Bruce Lee.

When he died on 20 July 1973, the world ended.

Sadness reigned. The world would never be the same again.

All was lost.

Elvis was the same story. Where would we find more perfection in this world? Who could be more talented, more unique, and more of all we wanted to be.

Yes, let them make fun of him. Let them call him fat and a has-been. But if Elvis was a has-been in later years, that only meant that the rest of us were never anything. Never.

He had his own style and it was all his own. He did not have to replicate anyone. He did not have to show anyone up or compete. He was Elvis and that was all that you had to say. He was Elvis, the one and only. There was a halo over his head. He walked on water. He did not drop down like the rest of us. He could not fall.

When he died on the 16 August 1977, again, the world ended. We never would be there again. No-one could ever replace him.

Bruce Lee and Elvis.

Forever.

When they left, the world was finished. When they left, we could never get them back. When they left, no-one could be happy again. There was just nothing to celebrate any more and they could not be replaced.

Were we stupid to care about them so much? Were we just simple and useless?

Were we wrong?

No. It was not a joke, and to so many of us they were heroes. There was just something about them. There was just something that could not be replicated and restored when they died.

Who do we have now?

No-one like them; that is for sure.

It's like young love or your first kiss. Or the first time you feel love.

Once it's gone, it's gone.

Bisbee Arizona.

A bright, sunny day in the desert. Skies so blue. You could see the Mexican border and there were no drones flying over or mafia murders.

What happened since then?

Clearly.

Elvis and Brue Lee had died.

He remembered he had gone with his first wife to visit a large, open, silver mine. Or maybe it was a copper mine or a turquoise mine. It was a sunny day. She had just come over from the east to visit him. They had an old used blue Toyota. They made the trip there.

They did not have credit-cards. They did not need money. They did not own a house. The injustices of the world did exist. They were not trying to figure everything out. They did not know so much and had not had time to think things through. It was a rare moment.

And the rare moment would never be repeated again. It was a crystal in the sun.

It was gone as soon as it had happened.

It was before he learned how to drink. It was before all was broken and rebuilt. It was another person. It was a nice day in the desert. He took her to see the mine.

Where did it all go?

Who was that person?

How amazing to live without disgust and regret. How amazing to wake up without feeling bad for what you had done. How amazing to look forward and not look back.

Mission Accomplished. A big banner.

Mission Accomplished. A big lie.

Mission Accomplished. A feeling of terror.

Because that is all we have left.

Mission Accomplished.

That is what life is. An ending, and not a beginning.

Yes our lives are just that: Mission Accomplished.

We run and run. Get this done and that. Remember this and that. Look back and feel the weight of all that we have done.

Mission Accomplished.

That was probably what Bruce Lee and Elvis did not have. They did not have to scream, "Mission Accomplished".

They did not have to water-board anyone.

They did not have to look back and categorize anything.

They accomplished everything without having to show what they had done. They were beyond this. They lived, without counting. They lived without some total. They were the total without having to mark it down. All that they were was obvious.

They were heroes. It was just that simple. And no, we were not stupid then. We are stupid now.

Forever, they would be together.

Shining examples.

Nothing more or less.

You did not have to say anything more than that.

Elvis and Bruce Lee.

Bruce Lee and Elvis.

Mission Accomplished, you did not have to say it. For once.

TWENTY

YOU WERE THE PEOPLE I HURT BY ALL THE THINGS I NEVER SAID, SHOULD HAVE SAID AND SHOULD NEVER HAVE SAID

All of them.
All of them.
All of them.
What I should have said and never did. Not the garbage that left from my mouth. Not the cruel and unnecessary words.
You were what I should have said.
Maybe it was an, "I love you."
Or maybe it was an, "It will be all right."
Or maybe it was, "Maybe we should say good-bye now."
There were just thousands of them.
When I said the wrong thing instead of the right thing, it was not what I should have said and it was most of the time.
What about the times I should have kept quiet instead? So many times. In fact, I now know that there were so many times, that I prefer not to speak at all. So many times I spoke, when silence was better, that now I don't even want to hear my voice anymore. These words were always my greatest regret. My words caused so much pain to so many.
So much pain, so many cruel words.
I was incredibly cruel, so many times.
But there were others. I was a coward. I could not say what I should have said, so many other times. People were depending on me. People were waiting to hear what really was in my mind, but I just let it go. I said nothing. Or I led them astray. They were waiting for me. Because I spoke so much, my silence was a lie. My silence was a knife. My silence was deception.
I let so many things go on for so long. I could not stop them. I kept silent about what was important and spoke of things that were not important at all.
I did all of this so I could avoid saying what I should have said. This was just as bad as the thousands of times I said too much or the wrong things.
I was terrible at communicating.

55

That was the sad thing. I thought I could speak so well and I did such a bad job of it all the time.

I really cannot put into words this grave error. I was so off so much of the time.

Yes, we all struggle with this. Yes, we all say too much, too little, or the wrong things. Yes, I am not the only one. But we lose so much because we cannot even talk to each other, or we never say what we should. Really we lose so very much.

Why did I never even think about how and why I was talking to people? Why did I struggle with such a basic skill? Why are so many of us crippled like this?

And.

Why do we hurt each other so much because of this?

I may never have this figured out. But, profoundly, it was one of the worst things in my life. We feel so much and express ourselves so poorly.

To those I hurt, thank you. I am learning to speak, very slowly. Your pain was the price. I am sorry. I was always, and continue to be, so inept. This is a struggle which for me will never end.

TWENTY-ONE

JAIL, DHARMSALA BLUES AND SADHUS

He looked out of the window.
She was gone.
He kind of missed her. She had added something to his day in gaol. Well, he was punished or maybe not. Maybe he liked his gaol. Quiet, it was. A good gaol. A silent gaol.
What is gaol, anyway?
He often thought gaol would be a liberating thing. No more responsibilities. You could not pay your bills there. No-one could ask you anything because, well, you were in gaol. Maybe people could visit you, but not get too close. You could not get any Swine Flu easily. There was food there too and books and they were so nice as to lock your cell at night. Maybe you could not look at anyone there but that was true on any Saturday night in London on the Tube. Danger was everywhere, on the road, on the mountain and even in space. It could get boring, he guessed, in gaol. But doing the same thing every day, or talking to the same people or seeing the same sights on your commute to the wonderful office could also get boring. Boring was really relative; ask anyone that. Really relative was the concept of boring. Truly relative.
And he liked to be by himself now.
Really, he did. He could relate better that way. His new job was just fine also, he could work at home. Maybe he could not overspend. But so what? Most of us on this planet cannot overspend. It was just a fact of life. Buy what, anyway? There were just too many chocolate bars; and eggs were really disgusting.
He suddenly thought of His Holiness the Dalai Lama.
Well, he was in the gaol of exile. Though who knows? Maybe he would have been happier in India, than Tibet. He was certainly a good traveller. Who knows? Really if it was his karma to go to India by horseback all those years ago, it was really how it was meant to be.
That was one great task in life. Saying, well everything is how it is supposed to be. Just accept it. Things are the way they are because things are the way they are. It is so simple. It was just because. You could not change everything everyday anyway. It was

impossible. If you were in a spot of bad luck, you could hope to change everything at once, but probably it could not be done. If you were in a good position, well everything could not go to hell right away, anyway. Or could it? Well, even if it could, the obvious answer was, things are the way they are supposed to be. If we could just get that into our heads, we would not spend all day thinking about how to get out of – or stay in – the situation we were in. Really, it was that simple.

And yes, the Dalai Lama was in India, because that was just how it was supposed to be. That's how it had worked out.

He had recently said that China was putting Tibet into a "Living Hell."

But how did that living hell compare to the living hell of Iraq or the living hell of Gaza or the living hell of Auschwitz or Treblinka (not the same camp of course, just the same purpose), or the living HELL of North Korea or Stalin's Russia? What about the living hell of the Christians in Kerala State in India, who were being burnt out of their homes by the orthodox Hindus?

What would the Dalai Lama say about that? Were all of these cases living hell also? Would he go and send all the Tibetans in exile to protest against the murder of the Christians in Kerala? Would he speak out about the living hell of the Palestinians in Gaza or the untold suffering of the Jews at Auschwitz and Birkenau (adjacent camps, for those who care anymore)? What would he say about Kashmir? – Really, on a universal scale it was all the same, wasn't it?

I mean, was this Dalai Lama going to be the last? Should he go back to China and be jailed, or be restored to his position, or whatever?

Was being in India going to save the Tibetan culture? Or was there going to be a Chinese Tibet and an exiled Tibet forever?

How could all this get resolved?

With the West in the living hell of economic destruction, who would save Tibet now?

Probably nobody.

It was just the way that it was.

One really great thing about India, anyway, was the sadhus. They are those guys who just give up on the world, leave their homes and just go wherever, sometimes without clothes. They just say, "Screw it all", and leave. They have no names, cheque accounts or places to be. They just give it all up.

That was probably a good solution and a gutsy one. – I mean it would be so hard just to let it all go. No more name. No more place. No more status. No more no more.

Being a sadhu was much harder to do than even going to gaol. They were really something. They just gave it all up. This was really quite a tradition. You had to stop and be amazed by the thousands and thousands who just wander around with no real aim other than to attain enlightenment. They were really something. No-one ever talks about them at all. We just talk about the Indian Cricket League or Mumbai, the Indian financial centre. These aimless ones were really the story but there are no words about them.

Maybe they were dead?

Maybe they were in gaol?

I mean you could see them. They were there. They were physical things. You could touch them.

But we never said a thing.

He looked back out of the window.

Maybe the girl outside was a sadhu and not a person having problems.

Can women become sadhus? – Which political party do they vote for?

Someone needed to explain exactly how all this worked.

Maybe the Dalai Lama could help with this?

Probably not.

TWENTY-TWO

YOU WERE ALL THE PLACES I NEVER WENT TO

I cannot be sure why I went where I went. It was never clear.

Equally, it was never clear why I never saw some places and missed others.

Vienna. – Wow the coffee must be great! – Never.

Cairo. – Well I would never visit the PharoahsPharaohs; we have enough of them on earth now. – Never.

Tripoli. – I really don't want to get in an argument with any of you Libyans. – Never.

I never got to see you. I never dreamed of you.

Riyadh. – Skip this one entirely! – Never.

I am sure you are beautiful places.

Venice. – You are supposed to go there with the love of your life. Count me out on that. – Never.

Maybe I thought I might be visiting all of you. I would have been happy to see all of you. Maybe I was missing something very important.

Moscow. – I have visions of big guys in leather coats at the strip clubs and I play very bad chess. – Never.

No. I take that one back. I think.

Helsinki. – I never even dreamed of it, and I don't want to get depressed about it. – Never.

Bangalore. – I would just be segregated into the rich upper-class of Karnataka State and forced to play golf. – Never.

Tupelo Mississippi. – I heard there are ghosts there. – Never.

Brighton and Brixton. – I will just pass. Rio sounds better. – Never.

Canada. – I missed the whole country. – Never.

Kampala. – I have seen pictures of Kampala; it is lush and green. – Never.

Kabul. – Well, that is off-limits now. – Never until next week.

You can't go everywhere. You can't miss everything and everyone. You get what you get.

I have always admired those who really want to go somewhere and they just go. I have always admired those who are content where they are and need nothing else.

We all end up somewhere between these two options. Some of us are happy where we are, but wonder what we missed. Some of us are miserable where we are and wonder how we got there. Some of us are just tired and do not want to go anywhere and learn it all again. There is a time-limit to learning every thing and every place.

Casablanca. – Another mixed-message city. Maybe after the Islamic Revolution. – Never.

Prague. – I hear it's beautiful but they always find themselves on the wrong side of history. – Never.

Jerusalem should be fantastic and spiritual and then again NOT. – Never.

Providence, Rhode Island. – Passed by once. Never had the pizza. – Never.

Hanoi. – Well I still call Ho Chi Minh City, Saigon. Sorry. – Never.

Darwin. – Was this place named after Charles Darwin from Ecuador? – Never.

Nairobi. – The riots and slums scare me. – Never.

Ulan Bator. – This one should be great. Should I speak Russian? – Never.

What did I miss? What did I have?

There is so much I never understood. All these places and languages I never learned. All that I never did is represented by all the places where I never went.

You can not meet all the challenges in life, or go everywhere. No-one can. Some figure this out faster and some much slower. Some go early and some go late.

At some point, I just kind of gave up on seeing all of you. Life was too tiring. I could not see all of you. Anyway, why go for a short time? You just see a little bit and never understand anything. It's like, "I just went to Barcelona, and I saw the sights."

Why do we do that anyway?

I saw the sights, then I left.

Was I ever there, and what did I find out about in three days or two weeks?

Why do we go anywhere?

I am not against being a tourist but what does it do for you and for them? You see a little and go home. You feel refreshed and can go back to your normal work? You saw a bit more of the world and understand more?

It was hard to figure out. This and thousands of other things.

Anyway, I never saw all of you, and every place. So, what did I do on this Earth?

I am not sure, and I am not sure I will ever figure all of this out.

Thank you. Even if I never went to this place or another place, you were there for me and I could have gone. That was freedom and a blessing which so many do not have. But would it have been so terrible never to have gone anywhere? I am just not sure.

TWENTY-THREE

PARQUE HUNDIDO – PYRAMIDS – SEŇOR ROJAS

Well of course it was the Swine Flu that was grabbing our attention. Might kill everyone or might just fade away. Terrorists, Swine Flu and a bankrupt Britain make for a good life these days. We are probably exhausted by all of this. No, we are not probably all exhausted by all of this. We are, in fact, all exhausted by all of this, and everything else.

So, there was a phone-call to make to his friend in Mexico. Really, that is the least you can do. He would call later.

Every time he thought of Mexico, two things came to his mind, pyramids and the Parque Hundido.

First of all, he would never visit pyramids. Never. It was clearly bad luck. You just don't go there. Nothing against them; but stay away!

In 1977, during the summer, he had gone on a trip to Mexico and met a German guy with a camera. The German guy invited him to come to the pyramids outside of Mexico City. He told the guy not to go. It was just not a place to go. The German guy thought he was crazy. He said something like, "Well, how can you go to Mexico and not see the pyramids? You really do not understand how to travel!"

Of course the German guy went anyway. And of course, he was beaten and robbed on his way back to the hotel. Now, clearly this was a case of, "I told you so." Never go to a pyramid. Rule Number One.

They travelled together later on a twenty-four-hour train trip to Oaxaca. He did admit later on that pyramid visits were not a good idea.

Another time he was in Cozumel. Same story, a young foul-mouthed American rich guy, and his girlfriend were sharing a house with him. They invited him to go and see the pyramids. He told them not to go because it was bad luck.

Of course the foul-mouthed guy was bitten by a scorpion while on the pyramid and contracted hepatitis the same week. What could he say? He wanted to laugh at them. But the poor jerk was so sick.

Don't go to visit the pyramids! They don't want us there. I am sure they are beautiful and fantastic and scenic, and meaningful and historical and all that. But just don't go!

Really, think about it. An ancient culture is reduced to a few sites. And we go to take pictures and be amazed. Just leave it alone. Let's just leave something alone. It is OK.

His favourite weird place in Mexico City was Parque Hundido, the Sunken Park. He knew where it was, because he used to stay in the Hotel El Diplomatico, which is located on Insurgentes Avenue, Avenida Insurgentes Sur. This was really a good one. He always stayed at the Diplomats' Hotel on the Insurgent Road. Insurgents are like terrorists and they need a road with a diplomatic hotel on it.

But that is just how Mexico is. They had a very long revolution during this century. They even have a Partido Revolucionario Institutional, a political party of the Institutional Revolution. But that party was in power for a long time and became definitely non-revolutionary after about sixty years in power.

The El Diplomatico Hotel was perfect. It was where all the people from the outlying states of Mexico stay when they are in the capital. If you do not understand this and the fact that the hotel has a certain name for this in Mexico, you would miss everything and think it was just a not so great or special hotel. But it has a reputation, and very important people from outside the capital like to stay there. You can hear different Spanish accents from the guests and not the Mexico City accent.

First of all, when you are in Mexico, always remember that for Mexicans breakfast meetings are really important. People like to have good meetings at breakfast in the morning at 7ish to 8ish. Breakfast is when business is done and plans made. Long lunches and drinking is more for long meetings with old friends, to discuss the world at a leisurely place. Dinners are for girlfriends or wives or couples or for weekends. Breakfast is the big meal of the day for getting things done. Famous restaurants for breakfast include VIPS and Sanborns or maybe they were the same company. Nice places for a business meeting and to start the day off right. This is how they do things in Mexico.

Now that was another secret of the Diplomatico. They had a great breakfast crowd. But you would miss this, if you did not know that the Diplomatico was famous for this too. It was probably a well-kept secret.

Also the Diplomatico has a great location. You can get around in the city quite easily from this location.

Across the street was Parque Hundido. This is probably the strangest park in the whole world. It is a park created in what really looks like a hole in the earth.

The Sunken Park in the middle of Mexico City.

It could be crowded and you still felt alone. It had pathways covered with trees and plants which sunk into the earth like some passageway to Hell. You were not sure how far down it was going to go. It went down quite a long way, always curving and always dark, even on a sunny day. There were many ancient statues from ancient periods of time like the Aztecs and even more ancient peoples. These and stone statues of other periods ring the park. Mexico has a very long history.

The first several times he went in the Park – usually in the day, after a breakfast meeting, because life slows down after breakfast in Mexico City – he felt the park might go all the way to the centre of the Earth. He was sure this must be the secret passageway. If you went to the bottom you would enter a hidden world of ancient gods, plotting their return from a long exile on the planet.

One day, after the cool Mexico City summer rain, he sat on a stone bench next to an old man. The bench was wet. The old man smiled. He had bright blue eyes and a white mustache, perfectly groomed.

"I was waiting for you."

"You were waiting for me, Señor. Why?"

"I am one hundred years old today."

He took out his Identification Card to show him. Sure enough his name was Jesus Rojas and it was his one-hundredth birthday.

"Well, Happy Birthday Señor Rojas. One hundred years is quite an accomplishment. What is your secret?"

"Well, my secret is, I have had over one thousand lovers. Because of this I have lived a full life and my health is perfect."

"Well, that is quite an accomplishment."

"Yes, and if you want to have a full life you should be like me. That is what I was waiting to tell you today."

"OK, that is a good idea, I guess."

Just then out of nowhere, came a tall blond beauty. She kissed Señor Rojas on the lips and – as she rained perfume on the whole world – said, "My Love, Happy Birthday. I am here. Let's go to celebrate your great accomplishment!"

Señor Rojas looked over at him, smiling, his eyes twinkling like the brightest stars at night and said, "You see, I was not lying and thanks for coming today. I was waiting for you. See you sometime."

Not knowing what to say, he replied, "Happy Birthday, and thanks for the advice. I will keep it in mind."

"Oh, I know you will."

Señor Rojas and the beauty left and proceeded toward the bottom of the park, quickly lost in the jungle-like vegetation. He stayed a while and did not see them go back up. Certainly they had gone together to the middle of the world.

Yes, the park was truly the entrance to another world. He was sure. It also had a very weird clock made of flowers at the front entrance.

Later he found out that the park was supposedly not the entrance to the middle world. It had been part of a brick mine belonging to the Noche Buena (Good Night) Mining Company and in the 1930s they had decided to make a park there.

But he did not believe it. Impossible.

Why name a mine, "Noche Buena"? Something was up. This was a real mystery and the truth would never come out. The Parque Hundido was really the entrance to the middle world. It was on a time-zone of its own and the old man was the king.

Just don't tell anyone! They might think that you were crazy.

Back to reality.

He called his customer in Mexico. Everything was OK. Thank God for small things and big things.

In the end, he was sure the flu would pass. And if it didn't he would still go to visit Parque Hundido once more. There he would meet his destiny, after breakfast at the Diplomatico Hotel, of course.

Hopefully, it would be before his one hundredth birthday. But judging from Señor Rojas' experience, maybe that was the place to be when you have been on earth for a hundred years.

But all those lovers? I might need some aspirin. I think I am getting a fever.

TWENTY-FOUR

YOU WERE SOMEONE I KNEW AND LOVED: TWO

This relationship never made any sense. We just could not get along. You pissed me off. You were always selfish. I gave and gave. We broke up and made up. We broke up again and you came back. I lent you money and you never paid it back. We broke up again and you came back. You said you had changed. You did not change that much.

I wanted to break up with you. You never let me. You wanted more than I could give. I never changed. I told you that I needed some time on my own. I did not want to be anyone's all the time. You said it was OK and then asked why I wanted to be alone, after I told you.

Every time you came back, you were more crazy and mood-swinging. The relationship was not that great. It was boring. We had nothing in common. I was your rut in the road of progress. You could never do anything on your own. You depended on me for everything. You would never let us break up. I really tried. But you knew that I was not going to tell you to get lost. I just don't do that. I never have. I try to get away from people by avoiding them and making excuses. I never just tell someone, "It's over." I am a coward that way. You knew it. So we just never broke up.

What do I need to do? Should I move to the moon or go into a submarine for six months without emails or a telephone? Then could we have separate lives? The moon always seemed like a good place for me.

I really can't say I hate you. I don't. I love you. You were a big part of my life. I would rather not see you. I was always fine when we broke up. But you were not. You really do love me and I know it. You were guilt- stricken by how badly you had treated me. You knew so much of it was you. You knew I could just tell you to go to hell but that I never would. You knew I had the power but would not use it. So it went on like this for a very long time.

You would never find a new track. I was the only track you could conceive of. I knew that I would have this burden forever. It was the perfect trap.

Because you are used to being with someone does not mean it is right. But also, because you are used to being with someone, it becomes part of your life. Some people do not change. Some people change a lot. So things just got stuck between us, and because you won't give up, it all carries on endlessly.

Thank God, I still have some time to myself, but I have to work for it.

Thank you. You love me. I know that. But quicksand loves me too when I am stuck in it. But yes, I love you, as miserable as it all seems. Let's see what happens. Your patience is endless anyway.

TWENTY-FIVE

VIOLENCE AND TAIWAN

He put on a movie. It was violent. There was a lot of killing. There was a lot of blood. For two hours he watched it. There was a hero. There was a villain. There were crowds and death. It was supposed to be entertaining. Maybe it was in a way. Maybe it wasn't.

We have some sort of ingrained love of violence. Or do we? We really crave it. Or may be we really detest it. Yes, there is yin and yang. Duality. Or is it love and hate. But where does watching pain come into this? It must hurt to get your leg destroyed. Hurt terribly. Or have bullets flying everywhere and all the body-tissue destroyed. It must hurt terribly. But we watch it anyway, as if we were watching a flower open or a couple discuss what house to buy.

That was a great movie.

That movie was too violent.

We kill and kill on the video screen. Some of us have game rooms to kill and kill on the video screen. Then we go to work in the morning.

Some of us kill and kill on the video screen and then we go out and buy real guns. Some of us – a growing number – go and kill and kill after we are frustrated.

Then we blame the police for being uptight.

There is something wrong. There is something wrong.

Do we want to fight all the time? Do we want to watch blood?

Are we OK in the head anymore? Any of us?

No, we are not. Two hours of endless violence is not alright for the head or heart or mind.

We are not OK in the head. Anymore.

The violence ended. There was an advertisement about Taiwan. It was terrible. It missed the point. Why do we need to spice up a place and make it fun?

Taiwan is fantastic. It is green. It has great food. It has nice and hard-working people. A stroll in the street will reveal miracles. You can see an old man practicing tai chi exercises. Then you will see ladies doing complex and intricate flower arrangements. Two houses from there, next to a small bookstore, you can see a young boy learning the violin and making honest mistakes as he progresses smiling in front of his teacher.

There is a smell of incense as you stroll by small temples and maybe start to sweat in the heat of the night. The bookstores are crowded and the young people sit in the aisles reading. It gets very quiet on most of the side-streets at night and you can see the restaurant workers in the alleys in their white aprons and hats smoking cigarettes during their breaks.

It rains a lot and you can hear the rain hitting the sidewalk, or falling slowly in big drops from the leaves of the very green trees; while yellow, Japanese-made, taxis pass by, always ready to stop. You can watch the crowds of motor-cycles drive past and see their red tail-lights fade away into the night, below neon signs that advertise everything. May be, at the same time, you will hear a plane flying low as it approaches the domestic airport at night, and think about all the people in the plane and where they are going and where they have been.

Taiwan is Taiwan, and Taiwan is wonderful. It has its own atmosphere. You cannot find this atmosphere anywhere else. Maybe it's the earthquakes or the typhoons, but there is a soft alive energy in the air.

The people have a calm fellowship together. They are friendly. They are very family-oriented. They care about each other and care that the luscious green rice-fields are well maintained. Taiwan is also famous for its fruit and you can get almost any fruit there.

A walk through one of the night-markets is unlike any other in the world. It is so alive and special, and you can share life with them, just as they live it themselves. Each stall is lit by a bright light-bulb and when they are all together, the market just shines into the night. Lots to buy, and great prices.

You can go for a massage that leaves you feeling like a new person.

There are tall mountains and waterfalls that most definitely spill bright sparkling water into caverns. There are hot springs and beaches which are connected by stone paths under big trees with bright yellow birds singing in the branches.

Taiwan is an island, surrounded by sea. You can sit on the west and look towards big China, and on the north and think about Japan and on the east and dream of America. You look out and it can all be there.

You can get seafood, spiced with soy sauce and pepper, just off the ship, and enjoy it while you watch the local neighborhood celebrate the local god in a bright fire-cracker-ringing parade and festival, as hundreds watch on the street.

Buddhist monks can be seen as they walk quietly in the night. You can wonder about them and what they are thinking, maybe they are not thinking at all and they are walking in meditation.

These are the kinds of things you can see in Taiwan. So many things to see and experience there and all are special.

Just think about what it would be like to spend a week in a small, clean, hotel, with a balcony looking out to the sea, and hear the sounds of the town. The children will be going to school in the morning in their uniforms and backpacks, and their mothers will watch them as they skip down the street toward the future.

You could just walk down the street and see what is in all the stores without buying anything; just to see. You might miss the sunset because of the clouds, or the sun might surprise you and come out all red and fall slowly into the sea. It is wonderful.

What else could you want?

Why can't a place just be a place? Why can't we just see it for what it is and see it for what is wonderful there? No need to make up anything. No need to fall in love, because if you see all that is wonderful, you will fall in love anyway. Taiwan is wonderful. It is alive. It is special. It has all it needs every day to be what it is. You could never ask for more and why would you?

No need to spice things up. Just tell it like it really is.

That is what the advertisement did not say and should have said. Maybe they wanted to explain better. Just maybe they were on a budget and could not say it all.

See a violent movie or see Taiwan? Just see Taiwan every time.

TWENTY-SIX

YOU WERE MY WORK, MY LABOUR AND WHAT I DID TO GET PAID

I am not sure I was very good at anything I did. I never really found something that I could say was my "passion" in life. I had a few jobs. I worked here and there.

Really I worked too hard. I was burnt out for most of it. I started working very young and at some point – to be quite honest – at some point, I really lost interest.

I had to pay my bills and take care of my children. That was really why I was working. That was really why. I did not ever find one thing that I liked so much that I became really attached to it. And even if I did, after doing the same thing for so long, I eventually lost interest in all of it.

I never felt very successful. I never felt very unsuccessful. I just kind of got by – not very well and not very poorly. Sometimes I was good, and at other times I could have worked much better. I felt at a loss a lot of the time.

I worked very long hours. But I did not get as much done as I could have. Thank God for the internet. I wasted a lot of time on this.

I never felt like I got the big break and I felt that I screwed up a lot of things. Maybe I did not deserve a big break, and I would have screwed it up like I did so many other things.

Others would look at me and say I was doing very well. I made it look like I was.

But the truth was neither one thing nor the other. I was not as good as I looked or as bad as some others. I could never say, except for some brief moments, that I was the best at anything. And I always felt so burdened by so much responsibility that I could never see a light ahead, or an escape, or a peaceful retirement, resting on my laurels.

The problem is, when you look like you are doing very well, people don't realize what you are doing wrong. You are the only one who knows how much you really fail.

I was never content with my work and labour. It is just a fact. I never got to the top of the hill and never could look down. I was always climbing and climbing.

I did sometimes see that others felt just the same as I did. They were tired too. They did not do everything right. They felt failure barking at their heels as I did. They failed also.

That realization did make me feel better. None of us, I realized, ever do all we want, or as well as we would wish. Life is hard for us all. We are limited, and often frustrated. Life wears us down and our work and labour are just what we do to get by. The higher or lower we climb, the harder it is to rise or fall.

Thank you. I am sorry I did not do better in life. I made too many mistakes. It is hard to feel fresh after so long in this life. Maybe be tomorrow will be a better day for us all. I hope I somehow can make a breakthrough in what has become so tedious and difficult.

TWENTY-SEVEN

SAINTS AND MARTYRS
ALIENS WEARING FACE MASKS

It was time to go out again. It was the first Wednesday of the month. Time to see Edgar and Jack.

Ah, Edgar and Jack!

It was funny. He had introduced them. And now they were best friends. It was funny. One was an ex-Catholic Priest and the other was an ex-Buddhist Monk. It was funny, they had once been alcoholics and he had persuaded them to stop drinking.

It was funny. He was now the monk and they were social animals out every day. It was funny. They claimed to see aliens and he knew – and they were sure – that he was an alien. And yes, he had seen aliens. But he never told them. Once when they were drunk in the past he had told them that he had seen ghosts. But they had forgotten about that.

The three of them would meet on the first Wednesday of every month, except on full moons, in a small bar on a small side street, with a big TV. He never really knew what they did for a living. Edgar was the ex-Buddhist Monk or so he said. Jack was the ex-Catholic Priest. They would talk for about an hour and watch the local TV comedy show for an hour and laugh. Then they would leave. It was like this every month. And it was quite fine.

"So are you still not talking, Mr Silence?" asked Edgar.

"Well, only when necessary. Did talk a little today," he answered.

"And you, Jack, how is the love affair with Jesus going?"

"Well, glad you asked. It is true. I fell in love with Jesus a long, long time ago. I have never stopped loving him. Even today."

"Which saint will you tell me about today?"

It was true. He made both of them talk about one saint or one enlightened one every time he met them. It was their penance, or duty or dharma or whatever. He had spent a lot of time with each of them in the past, when they were down-and-out alcoholics. He had harassed them until they just stopped drinking. It was one of his finest moments. Now they could sit in a bar, and not drink and be just fine. And all they had to do was tell him about one saint or one bodhisattva or some holy one.

He never knew much about them really, other than the story of their lives that he had heard when they were drunks. So he knew everything and nothing at the same time. They were weird. After they were not alcoholics, they never talked about what they had done in the past or why they left their religious orders. It was as if all he had known had vanished. Now he was not sure if he ever knew anything about them. It was all a dream.

Jack was the one who had recommended that he meet Mr Kim, the defector, in Korea. Other than that, they shared little with him. It seemed they shared more with each other, but he could not be sure.

"Well, Mr Silent, your saint for today is Saint Martin of Tours. Saint Martin in his youth was a Roman soldier, who declared that he would fight only for God. One famous act of his was when he saw a poor man on the street, he tore his beautiful Roman robe in half and gave it to the poor man and went on his way with only one half of his clothes.

"He was later to become the Bishop of Tours in France, but refused to live in a palace and moved to the outskirts of the city to live in a cabin made of branches. He was determined to convert the non-Christians of the area and went from house to house with his disciples, working for their conversion. We really cannot understand today the devotion of the early Christians. It was quite a special movement in its time. They were willing to sacrifice themselves for their beliefs, no matter the cost. That kind of devotion is very hard to find any more."

"Well, Jack, the Moslems are doing some pretty extreme and devout things these days!"

"Yes, you are right. I need to think about that much more. Well, back to the Saint. He was also famous for working to save prisoners from death and torture. He was big on destroying the temples of the pagans.

"But he was human and made mistakes and he was hard on himself. Before he died, as he was contemplating his mistakes, an angel said to him, 'Take courage in yourself. Regain your firmness, so that you do not imperil your own glory and salvation.' His feast day is the 11th of November, and he was buried in an unmarked grave in a paupers' cemetery.

"Is that enough for today? You know I need to study these things for you."

"Yes, thanks, Jack. That was a good one."

"Edgar, and you?"

"Well, Silent One, let's discuss the Maitreya Buddha. He is the one who has not yet arrived. We are all waiting for him to come. When he arrives, the world will enter a trance and we will all be able to go across the river of existence to the side of the enlightened one. He is now sitting in the Tusita Heaven waiting to attain the final Buddha state and we can communicate with him now. When he comes we will all live in the Ketumati Pure Land.

"When will he come, Edgar?

"Well, we cannot really say. He will come to save, the day when all the teachings of Gautama Siddhartha, our first known Buddha, are forgotten. He will come when we have forgotten all that is good and the seas themselves have dried up and we are all in a very bad state. He is the last card in our eternal struggle from good to bad and back again. Some believe that he is now again on the Earth. In fact, he is, to many, our final hope and we all must await his return."

"What do you think?"

"Well, Silent One, I am really not capable of telling you. I am just trying to get through each day. You know, you are a better teacher than you are a follower."

"What do you mean?"

"Well you helped us, but it seems you can't help yourself."

Not to miss a chance, Jack then chimed in, "Yes, Mr Silence, you are pretty oblivious, but we love you."

"Ah, oblivious, I have heard that before, dear sirs. I have heard it several times this week already. And I can assure you that I am on the road of non-obliviousness this week. So you missed your chance. Anyway, I know you just love to be with me, because I am the only one who can make you two look good. All good points though, and well taken. Thank you. Class is over. Let's watch TV."

They nodded. They smiled. And everyone watched the nightly comedy show. Everyone in the show seemed a bit nervous, as if the jokes were falling flat and the actors were afraid to be too close to each other. It must have been the swine flu affecting everyone. And the advertisements on the channel were all about making sure everyone washed their hands. A short news bulletin showed thousands of people wearing face-masks on a street in some city.

Jack said he thought they were not people but really aliens because the people were quarantined in their houses. Edgar agreed. But the real truth was that aliens can be seen only at dusk or at night. That was when they were out. He did not bother to tell them that. He did not want to ruin the comedy show or another night of sobriety for them.

After one hour, they got up, shook hands, and left.

They would meet again in one month.

As they were leaving, Jack said, "Oh by the way, the defector, Mr Kim, liked you very much.

"He did? Well, we mostly talked about the World Cup and soccer. I learned nothing except that South Koreans like to dance."

"Yes, that is why he liked you so much. He said he wants to see you again next time he is town. And he said he had left you a book, about Richard Sorge."

"Oh."

TWENTY-EIGHT

YOU WERE ALL THE THINGS THAT WENT RIGHT IN THE WORLD

This list is so big as to be ridiculous. For all that goes wrong, so many things always go right. Every time a plane takes off it is a miracle. Every time a child is born it is a miracle. How we manage to drive down the road without crashing all the time is a miracle. Buildings that don't fall down and bridges that cross great bodies of water are miracles. Electricity and wireless, the internet. The fact that so many of us are safe from diseases that ravaged us for centuries is a miracle.

So much goes right every day, we never notice. We are too busy thinking about our problems to see just how right so much is. The sun rises the next day, and the moon comes out full in its splendour. Children learn arithmetic and teachers struggle with good hearts to teach them. People put loving care into their shops and businesses, producing things to share with all of us.

It is not all black. It is not all grey. It is so much that is special. A smile from a stranger is special. An "excuse me" on a crowded train is special. Two people in love is special. When the mail arrives from a distant place it is special or when we make a long distance call it is special. Oranges from Mexico arriving fresh in China is special. Our birthdays and baptisms are special. The wise words from an older person trying to help are special. A night of silence and the sound of the rain are special.

Funny, so much is just so right, and funny we cannot see it. These are all the miracles of our lives and they are there every day. We just can't see a thing. It is normal. Miracles are boring. We just cannot sit in awe of each and every one.

I have been blessed by so many of these miracles. They are countless. I was so lucky and had so much. I saw so many changes for the good in my short life. I saw a million or more miracles. I never stopped to feel amazed by what I was seeing. So many blessings just lost to my oblivious nature. So much softness, so much freedom, so many things that no-one should miss, I never could see them.

What was I thinking? Or rather, why could I never think?

If I could now, I would stop and shout with joy for every blessing. Every time I ate food or drank water and turned on the lights in my room, I would do so. These are clear and wondrous miracles and blessings that we do not recognise. They are blessings I took as nothing. So much went perfectly for me. Constantly and daily I lived a blessed life. Countless blessings; yet daily I never saw you.

Thank you. So much was perfect and so much I never saw. I promise I will start now to stop and notice you all and in silence scream my appreciation. I need to scream now, because I was without a word of praise for so long. I hope you can hear me screaming. It is really about time.

TWENTY-NINE

COUPLES IN LOVE – NGO DINH DIEM

After the one hour meeting with Jack and Edgar, he had another monthly meeting with the La Barres, a nice couple from France. He had known them for a long time. Indeed, he was never quite sure why they liked him so much. Maybe they needed someone to talk to. Or maybe they were tired of talking to each other. Perhaps they had so much to say that he was a good recipient for the great amount of knowledge that they had.

Being with couples is funny. Are they two people or one? I mean, do they take on one personality or two? Is one person the dominant one, the decider? Or do they just meld into one person through the stretch of time that they are together? He really did not like being with couples anymore. He was never sure who he should talk to. Normally for a couple, you would be best friends with the man member of the couple, but you still had to talk to the wife. Or they would take turns telling their stories to you. It was really quite tiring anyway.

In any case, the La Barres were one person. Yes, you could see two life-forms in front of you, but in reality it was just one person. Yes, they were born at different times to different mothers, and maybe would die at different times. But they were now one person. Talking to Jean the husband with his longish grey hair, parted in the middle, was exactly the same as speaking to Marie the wife with her dyed blond hair and gorgeous, red, manicured nails. This must be what the greatest love is about. When you become just like someone else. It could be like being one with someone; your wife, or Jesus, or the Buddha or Chairman Mao.

They could both start and end each other's sentences. They had merged into one person. It was just obvious. Usually when he was with them he was trying to find out where the operation that had separated them had occurred. But no, they had just become one. So though it was a bit trying to talk to them, he finally figured it out and just spoke to them both at the same time, never knowing who would answer. It did not matter. What one said, was always the same as the other.

"Oh it is Jude the Obscure."

"Yes, Jude the Obscure. Do sit down."

"Yes, do sit down."

"I was just thinking about when I was young and met Ngo Dinh Diem."

"Yes it was Ngo Dinh Diem, when he was in the United States. Before he was President of South Vietnam."

"And he was so nice. You know Vietnam had a chance with him. It was just awful what the Americans did when they plotted to kill him. The war ended that day."

"Yes, ended and terribly. I remember when we were with him. That was before we met Reza Pahlavi when he was the Shah of Iran."

"Yes, Mohammed Reza Shah. We went to his party at Persepolis. Really quite a show."

"Really quite a show! We shared a drink with Elizabeth Taylor. And Empress Farah sent roses from Tabriz to our room at the Royal Pavilion."

"Yes Elizabeth Taylor! You have never seen such sparkling blue eyes. What a beauty."

"What a beauty! Like when we met Princess Diana."

"Yes, what a beauty! She said she thought the Royal Family were like lizards."

"Yes, lizards! We did not know what to think about it. But maybe be she was drunk."

"Yes, maybe she was drunk. Not that we did not like Dodi Fayed."

"Yes, we liked him too. We are good friends of his father. Oh, the tragedy!"

"Yes, what tragedy!"

"But what is tragedy, but an opportunity, I sometimes think."

"Yes, that is what Shimon Peres told us once. He is our friend."

"Yes, our friend. We shared a bottle of Rothschild wine with him at the kibbutz that time."

"Yes, at the wonderful kibbutz. Oh, you should have seen the grapes!"

Jean stopped to take off his sunglasses and replace them with his bifocals. Marie did the same thing. He finally got a word in.

"Do you think Karzai in Afghanistan will become the next Ngo Dinh Diem?"

"Good question."

"Very good question."

"Just remember that Ngo Dinh Diem was celibate, and Karzai is not."

"But that was a good question."

"Yes, a very good question."

"We met Hillary Clinton in Bosnia too. We are not sure if she is celibate!"

They both laughed. The same laugh together with the same volume.

"Yes, we are not sure if she is celibate!!"

They laughed again. The same laugh. The same volume. They were so happy with this statement.

In the background some music came on. It was "Autumn" by Vivaldi. Yes. It was so predictable. Autumn had two meanings. It was the season after summer and yes, it was a season of life. Like, after you are forty years old, you enter the "autumn" of your life. You picture leaves falling down and the weather getting colder by the minute. Then it is winter. Snow on the ground, freezing weather, the trees dark like the birches in the winter dark of the Ural Mountains, and yes, death before the renewal of spring.

But it didn't make sense. Some of us have winters before our summers, and some of us never have spring. Some winters are followed by autumn and then by spring, and some places only have two seasons. Summer can be long or short.

They spent the rest of the evening discussing the pros and cons of the Island of Bali versus the Island of Java in Indonesia. But it was really one conversation. It ended when the one person in the form of two said, "Well we need to go, but when I see the blue water of Bali I can never forget the stunning blue of Elizabeth Taylor's eyes. We will see you again next month. We just love to be with you. It is like eternal summer."

"Yes, we just love to be with you – an eternal summer."

"Oh yes, precisely, eternal summer."

"I feel the same way, Jean and Marie. I always do."

THIRTY

YOU WERE ALL OF THOSE I HATED

This was one of my great skills. Hate. Envy. Jealousy. I am not sure when I started to hate. I think I was not that old; probably a child. I remember I was a bully sometimes and I enjoyed it. One day, I brought a small boy to our house and urinated in his chocolate milk and made him drink it. Another time I stole another child's baseball cards. I did not kill cats or torture animals but I would on occasion torture other humans cruelly.

I guess that qualifies as hate.

What is hate? Is it when you see someone gulping their coffee in the morning and it just grates you the wrong way? Is it when you see someone with more than you, and you are jealous of what they have and what you do not have? Is it when you see someone on TV and you just want to kick the TV-set? Is it when you cannot get along with someone and their slights burn your heart and soul?

Most of it is illogical, of course.

Some of it is logical. Like when you hate someone or a group because they killed your family or your child.

But none of that ever happened to me. So it was always illogical and ridiculous for me.

Some of my favourite hates were brilliant criticisms of me made by other people.

Once, a guy that I worked with had me really figured out and said about my work performance at a new site, "Well they really like you here, but that is only because they don't know you yet."

And that is all he said. And he walked away after that.

And well, I have hated him for that comment for over twenty years. And it stung so badly, I really am just waiting for him to die, wherever he is.

Yes. When I hate, I just wait for them to die. The sooner, the better.

I can't beat them, I can't join them. That comment and others just crushed me. And every once in a while it comes back to me. And I do try to stay away from situations, so that I can prove that what he said is not true. But sadly, it was somewhat true and sometimes still is. That is why I hate him still. It was just too true.

Maybe it helped me, but I guess I still hate him, but less. And he will die anyway.

My hate was always like that. Someone who showed me up or did better than me or who was more handsome and whom others liked more or thought was smarter than me. It was stupid and meaningless hate.

Really, just little things, which I blew up out of proportion.

If someone really messed me over, I really did not hate them. It was more that I was confused about why they did it.

So I hated those I could.

At some point, I just realized that I was not going to win anything here on Earth. I still exhibit the symptoms of hate but it is really much less. I just got so much more love than I deserved and got away with so much more than I should have, that it did not make any sense to hate with such passion.

But it still does well up in me from time to time. But it does not flash from the heavens any more; it is more like a blue neon beer-sign in the dark of a late-night bar. It is not that I have improved so much. More likely, I am defeated. Life has won me over, via defeat and impending death.

Thank you. I should never have hated you. I was blessed. You really did nothing to me. It was insane and more than stupid of me to hate you. And the sad part of it all was, I really never even said anything to anyone about it. It was all internal until today.

THIRTY-ONE

BREAKFAST WITH THE PASDARAN IN LENINGRAD

After a couple of days of silence, he left the house again for a breakfast meeting. It was for another article on the Middle East. He wanted to talk to an Iranian and he went there with his friend, Vladimir, who said he worked for Novosti, the Russian news network.

Vladimir was everything wonderful about Russia. He was smart, handsome, and played great chess. He was not on the top of the corrupt food-chain but was climbing rapidly. And yes, he was a friend.

What is a friend?

It is someone you can go out with and talk and stay with until the early morning and someone who defends you in bad situations.

Vladimir just went with him because he was a friend.

They went to the coffee-shop to meet the Iranian. This was another of Jack, the ex-priest's strange contacts. The Iranian's name was Faraz Hussaini and apparently he was in the boat-repair business.

"Good day, Mr Hussaini."

"Oh you are Jack's friend. And I hear you never speak and just write articles now."

"Well, if Jack said that, it must be true. I speak only sometimes. And I don't write very much. I also sleep a lot now. But it's very nice to meet you."

"Well, we in Iran do admire silence. We think it takes a lot of silence to find something important to say. So that is why I agreed to meet you today."

"Thank you. This is Vladimir, my good friend from Russia. He works for Novosti."

"Nice to meet you, Vladimir."

Mr Hussaini stopped and rubbed his eyes. From his white shirt pocket he produced a small bottle of eye drops. And rubbed his eyes again. You could see two small scars by the side of his eyes.

"Are your eyes hurting you, Mr Hussaini?" Vladimir asked.

"Well, yes. In fact they always do. As a young man, I was gassed during the war with Iraq. And now my eyes always hurt, especially in the morning."

"Were you a Revolutionary Guard?"

"Yes, Jack was right. I am surprised you know about us. Yes I was a Pasdaran, but you could hardly call us much at all. I was just one of thousands of sixteen-year-old boys sent to the front to defeat the Iraqis. We weren't really very much of anything, just young boys without weapons. We were mustered to a train, given uniforms and a Koran, and sent through the night. I entrained with my friends in Tabriz. We didn't even know where we were going when we left the station."

"Which front did you go to?"

"I never was sure; it was a desert wasteland. I know I was injured near Susangerd when the Iraqis launched their first gas attacks in 1984. I will never forget the boys coughing out their lungs and the screams as we were evacuated. I could hardly see, but somehow I saw and felt it all. We were all in hell and pain."

"Did you want to be a martyr?"

"I was not sure about anything. I did not know what war was. We said we wanted to die. We were willing to die. We volunteered to die. Paradise, what was that? I know now, but did not then."

"What do you mean?"

"Well, we were just fighting for our country. We were getting crushed, bombed and gassed. We lost over one million souls in the war. We have a martyrs' cemetery in Tehran, where many of the friends of my youth are buried. It is a sad place and the fountains run red water. But you know, it is our place of victory. We were not afraid of death and we were ready to die. They lost their youths and I was hurt, but I am still here, as you can see. And I miss them. But we together in our innocence did not fail either Iran or God. So, in my life after that, nothing else matters and I am happy somehow. There was just something so poetic about it. When Ayatollah Khomeini died on 3 June 1989, we all cried."

Vladimir was listening closely in his so very intelligent way and then spoke up. "You know, Mr Hussaini, I am from Saint Petersburg, which was Leningrad during World War Two. We have exactly the same feeling. We were starved for nine hundred days, surrounded on all sides. The bodies of those dead from starvation were stacked in the street. But there was something special there. It was to us then and today a heroic city. I am sorry they changed the name. For me in my heart it is always Leningrad, the City of Heroes."

Mr Hussaini smiled but continued to rub his eyes in pain. He coughed twice.

"Vladimir, what do you think about Stalin?"

"Well, my friend. It is hard to say. I am sure Mr Hussaini feels the same way. There is something about being so defeated and crushed and rising up. We know Stalin was terrible. My Grandfather was imprisoned in the gulag. But when you overcome so much, you can somehow see the most terrible things in a different way. That is why we don't know how to answer questions sometimes."

Mr Hussaini smiled again.

Everyone smiled. And they ate together in silence.

Mr Hussaini looked happy indeed, suddenly almost radiant. He shook their hands at the doorway and commented, "Do say hello to Mr Kim when you see him. I hope you enjoyed the book he sent you. Have a wonderful day. Thanks for reminding me of the best time of my life. Good bye."

"Oh. OK. Thank you."

THIRTY-TWO

CHENGDU IS PARIS,
TATOOS THAT MEAN SOMETHING
A GREAT ENGLISH LESSON

The next day he had a plane-ride to make. The Swine Flu, now renamed H1NI, was raging. But he passed the temperature test at the airport.

But then again, he had no problem with the idea of quarantine. A week by himself, with food and TV, was hardly suffering. Everyone would be very nice and he had everything he needed with him. Vitamins, the list of Chinese Emperors, and an autobiography of Winston Churchill, in case he wanted to sleep. And quarantine guaranteed he would not infect anyone else. All for a good purpose, he thought, and not a problem at all.

He was going to Chengdu, Sichuan. Chengdu was the Paris of China and Sichuan was just as beautiful a province as God could put on this earth. The people were stylish, the weather was calm and they had so many restaurants on each street in Chengdu, you could just not count them.

The place is green, green, green. They grow gardens on the top of the apartments; lush green gardens. The trees grow very fast. A few years pass and they overhang the small streets, so that the pedlars and their bicycles can take breaks under them in the afternoon when business is down, and play cards. The children are happy, and their grandparents wait for them every day at 4pm when school gets out.

Chengdu is Paris. Sichuan is heaven. It was the truth. Chengdu will one day be known as the most beautiful city on earth. It is destined.

It has a beautiful, modern road-network with three ring-roads and huge, fantastic and very old parks, where the retirees dance together in the evenings all over the city. Why work when you can drink tea in the park and talk and have delicious hot-pot in the evening with your friends? Everyone likes to eat out and the restaurants are full, seven days a week. There is some rushing in the morning but really not much. Everyone just works at a nice pace, and you never really get a rushed feeling. The place has style –

twenty-four hours a day. This is the truth. It is ancient and very modern at the same time. It is heaven on earth.

And he loved Chengdu for all that, and much more.

And it is green, green, green. And the people are fashionable and friendly. It is Paris. And the food is amazing. The women are also beautiful and delicate and well-dressed.

Well, Chengdu was still two hours off and the plane had been delayed because of some bad weather in Guangzhou. He just hated how they load you onto the plane these days and have no problem keeping you there for hours, when they could just let you out for a while. It would all be the same in the end.

He had just stretched out in an empty section of the plane when three guys came and asked to sit with him. He really wanted to say no, but when they snarled a bit and flashed their tattoos at him in such a dignified way, he knew he really did not have a choice. Then they smiled as if they were somehow used to getting their way. As they sat down he saw the huge scars on their heads from past fights and could see the gold on their hands and the vibrant green and red dragon tattoos. He wanted to avoid it, but the Sichuan mafia was on the plane.

He wanted to be irritated by them. He hoped for about twenty minutes that the anti-crime team would enter the plane and take them away. But the plane was not moving and it was weather and not them that was causing the delay. He stayed irritated for a while. Then he remembered he was not supposed to hate.

In life, as in politics, and as in war, you need to remember who the enemy is. He analyzed the world around him and thought to himself this time, "Hey, these guys are not the enemy, I think." That was the first time he had ever thought that way.

He turned around to one of them and really studied him. He was handsome in a rough sort of way and rich in a three golden rings, two bracelets, and one golden-brand cell-phone way. He grabbed onto one of the guy's golden bracelets and said in Sichuan dialect.

"Hey, that is one great bracelet."

The guy answered in perfect English, "Thank you very much."

He answered again in Chinese, "You can speak English?"

"Yes of course. I learned a bit in school and I like it."

"But, you guys?"

"Us guys, what?"

89

"You know."

"Oh, you are so smart. Yes we just came here for some work. But I like English. I always study English. Look at this! I was working on this."

He handed him a big sheet of white paper with the words, "Xihua University" at the top.

He looked at it a moment and could not believe his eyes. There were a thousand small and perfectly-written words. The handwriting was perfect and the words perfectly spelled. It was a random list. He noted some of the words. Or it wasn't the words, or the randomness. It was the order of them.

One example was:

Suffer operate be on good terms direction brake cyclist fortunately drive off silence

Look on as rude confused unfair customer avoid contact frown lean suitcase ahead

Give somebody a hand fold very disrespectful thumb index crazy part Russia firm

Hand shakes interpretation palm put down and get through tear down shrug incredible

forefinger fist bend gently held up anger useless narration detail in order occur focus

specific table teenager run out in order file folder drugstore helpful tax modesty upset

ignored senior slice ability non existent chill indifferent sum up compete Asian

financial accumulate ancestors think up in the meantime career demonstration

He looked at the brilliant, successful gangster with a bow of respect. "This is just fantastic work. Your hand-writing is better than mine. What is it?"

"Just some words I was practicing. I do this when I have time."

"It is like poetry. – Really!"

"Poetry? How do you mean?"

"Well, words are like numbers and when you put them together they might mean something somehow and mean different things to different people. If you put these words together to me, they are like poetry."

"So in English you can mix words without any meaning and they might mean something?"

"Yes, sometimes it works like that. You are quite a student."

"Thanks. I will give this to you. If there are any problems with the words let me know. Here is my number. When we get to Chengdu, call me up, and I will take you out to our whorehouses as my guest."

They exchanged numbers. He looked at the dragon-claw and the scars on his hands as he put his number in the guy's golden phone.

"What is your name?"

"Golden Snake – Mr Tsong, to you."

"OK, Golden Snake, I am honoured to meet you, and glad we are together. Now I won't feel so lonely on the flight. I guess being with you guys is a great way to spend the time on the plane."

"That is why we sat here, you looked so very lonely."

"Oh. – What does that tattoo mean?"

"Well I can't tell you now, but all of our tattoos mean something. They are not like the play-tattoos some of you foreigners wear. We wear them as brothers and in memory of friends and things that happen to us. Each one has a meaning to us. Maybe, as we get to know each other better, I can tell you and you can help me with my English. And if you need something some time from me, or you need us to beat up someone for you, just ask."

"Oh, OK. I will call you."

It was a great flight that day. Chengdu is Paris and only two hours away; the soon-to-be-recognized most beautiful city in the world and Golden Snake the poet, and three new exciting friends. What more could you want?

THIRTY-THREE

YOU WERE SOMEONE I KNEW AND LOVED: THREE

I really wish you were just one person. But you are not. There are several of you and you merge together in my memory. You went from bright to grey to greyer until I can't really see you.

But I remember all of it in grey.

At first I really admired you. You know I did. I looked up to you. I thought you were everything I needed in one person, and that you could solve all my relationship problems. You were the love I needed. I was crazy about you.

One of you said I was like chewing-gum in the sense I just stuck to you. Another one of you asked why I gave you so many phone-calls. One of you moved away to avoid me. One of you I only saw for two weeks during one year. One of you, I would make long airplane journeys to see and then you had only a few hours to see me because you were "busy".

I wish all of you were not the same story. But you were. I fell in love so strongly and pushed so hard and in the end there was nothing. Not that I never came to this realization. I did. I did and then I was fine. It was just that it usually took over a year for the passion and desire to wane, and I lost a lot of time and effort on something that never really happened.

I would walk along the ocean and think of you, and point my face in the direction of where you were, and will something so strongly, and nothing resulted. I would lose weight in the vain attempt that you would somehow like me more. I would see the stars and think we were sharing them together. Once I told one of you that we were always under the same sky. So I believed at the time.

I always thought it would work out. I thought we would be together forever.

For some reason I craved these hard roads and impossible situations. I thought I could just will them along. I could enforce a reality that was never going to be.

I am not sure. We always started so strong. We got along fine. Then the break came and I was unaware till months later that nothing was there.

I was completely unaware.

One of you did come back after about two years, and I really didn't like you any more. It was over. You did not look so special any more. I am not sure what you were thinking. You can not fill up a crushed aluminum can again. It is crushed. You crushed me. It was as if you did not even remember the day. I still do.

For the rest of you, it is the same. I was crushed. I recovered. I loved and I lost. It is alright when it ends. The pain even goes away. Amazingly, the pain even goes away.

Every time, I said it would be the last time.

I am not sure that you were the best choices that I could have made. You seemed to be at the time. I really tried. Not one of you can say that I did not give it my all. You know I did. I would be willing to bet that you have never met anyone like me again. Maybe it is for the worst or for the best. I am not sure. I could never seem to penetrate your hearts, or conquer them, or be the one you wanted at the time. But I cannot be sure.

I have the faint hope still, somewhere, that all my great efforts were not completely lost in the eternity of this cosmos. I somehow believe that the prayers and hopes and the endless hours I spent thinking about you and all the pains I suffered when I was crushed are still out there somehow. After all, I was crazy about you.

So in love!

In a funny way, I wish someone would treat me the way I treated you. It still has not happened.

Thank you. I wished so many times you were the one for me. It did not work out. I was a fool and learned a hard lesson. But you know, in the end, I am not afraid of losing. The effort was worth it. So I want to believe. I am not giving up. Just like back then, I am not giving up. So I want to believe.

THIRTY-FOUR

COUPLES IN LOVE: TWO – MINIATURE GOLF

There was a television show on about John Lennon and Yoko Ono.

Then it hit him. That *was* a couple in love. There was just something so special about them. The way they looked at each other. There was a knowing stare of complete love. Yoko playing the drums in a serious way at his side was a constant sight. She was so serious, she was so sincere. John was so honest. Forget it; that was a great couple. They stood together. Maybe they had some bad times, we all do. But they stood together. And, because they stood together, they never fell.

Yes, they were a couple in love.

What about John Lennon. Is he being forgotten?

Maybe.

But, you know, after all these years, he was right. A world without borders. Give peace a chance.

Are we all cynical now?

Maybe there wasn't room for dreamers. But truly his heart was in the right place. Have we all given up?

Maybe if he had lived, he would have done advertisements for Apple computers. May be age would have ruined him. Or may be we lost a saint. Yes, he was a rich saint. But he was a saint because he refused to give up dreaming about what we could be as humans. It was worth it.

Have we forgotten him? And then?

Peace as a concept is dead. Peace as a desire is dead. Movements for peace are dead. We have lived through thirty Vietnams since the War in Vietnam. Nothing is said. We just go along with it and oppose war as if it was just another opinion. Progress is not a concept; it is a viewpoint. It is not what is right, or wrong. We do not stop our daily schedule for peace. We just go about things as normal every day. We can't find our way. John Lennon could find his way. He knew how to be lost. We don't have a clue.

John Lennon! He needs an institute.

John and Yoko deserve a statue in New York.

His sayings need to be repeated and repeated every day. They made sense. He was not a fool; he was correct. He could turn our logic on its head and he could see beyond it.

The way they looked at each other. The courage of their love was immense. It was courage. It was not crazy.

Fear is crazy. Compliance with immorality is crazy.

People think it is funny; but dedication, caring and love were there. Give them a round of applause and listen again to their words and the song of their lives together. You won't need to contradict them. You will never need to reject them again.

He got a call from the United States. A friend was inviting him to visit Chicago.

They were in the middle of the conversation, when the friend said, "Hey, we can go get drunk and play miniature golf. That doesn't take much talking. You will like that."

"Well, I really don't like to drink in the States."

"Why?"

"Well the police have guns and tasers and they use them. I am afraid to drink there. Something might happen."

"That is true. But do they have miniature golf in China?"

"Well, not yet; but they are getting automatic car-washes."

"Well, that is what I am talking about."

"What?"

"Miniature golf and guns go together. You can't have miniature golf unless the police have guns."

"It's like a parallel universe thing. Is that it?"

"Exactly! They would never have miniature golf in a place where the police don't carry guns."

"Well it's not very scientific; but somehow, strangely enough, it sounds plausible."

"So who is your favourite guitarist?"

"John Mclaughlin and the Mahavishnu Orchestra, and not Santana."

"Good choice!"

"Well I can't say Santana, but what about Cheech and Chong."

"Cheech and Chong don't play guitar."

"But they might play miniature golf and carry guns?"

"Oh, that makes sense!"

"Let's just see the Rocky Horror Picture Show together."

"OK, sounds like a plan!"

"You're sure you don't want to play miniature golf?"

"No. Now every time I think about it, I will think about guns, thanks to you!"

"Yeah, I can see your point. What about go-karts?"

"Gets me dizzy, but we could watch racing on TV. That sounds safe."

"Yes, that is what we will do then."

"OK, sounds like a plan."

"Do you feel better now?"

"Yes, I do feel better."

"OK. Bye, see you soon."

"Bye, it was nice to talk about this."

"I thought you would like it."

"Oh."

THIRTY-FIVEE

YOU WERE MY FRIENDS

Oh what an unlucky group! You really liked me. What does that say about you?

You listened to all my crazy, overdone talk. You defended me in tough times and always helped me.

I really never wanted to see any of you all the time. I would disappear. I would go to my silent place and not see you for months or years. If I was having a hard time, you would not hear from me. I was always really insecure with you. I loved to turn off my telephone. I loved to go to one place and then go somewhere else. I did this to absolutely everyone.

Did I really trust anyone?

Probably not.

I could not imagine that I could share everything with anyone. I loved to disappear too much. I loved to move around. I loved to be the loner. I knew that I was born alone and would die alone. I did not take this fact lightly. Friends were just that – friends. I did not want to go all the way on any path with anyone. Sure, I missed something; but I also gained.

I had feelings for you, for sure. But I thought life was really a tough climb and tiring. I am irritated when tired and miserable and really did not want to share my misery with you.

I guess it's called partitioning. I separated myself from everyone. Everyone had one space, sometimes I was there and sometimes I was not.

That is just how I chose to live.

Sure it hurt. We all want to be together.

And sure you made the pain less when you were there. But I would never let anyone be there all the time.

I am not sure why.

I guess I was afraid.

But in the end I am not sure I was worse than anyone. I think we are all somewhat the same. We separate. We don't go too far. We keep things at one level. We hope that everyone can feel our pain, but we are not sure and do not want to impose our problems on anyone else. We essentially live alone all the time. Our hearts beat by themselves. We breathe in our own air and think our own thoughts. It is impossible to read each others' minds. We have enough trouble, thinking our own thoughts and feeling our own emotions.

How can we get so close to each other?

We never go that far.

Friends or not, it is so limited. We are so separated from each other. We do not want to admit it but that is how it is for all of us.

Thank you. I had the friends I had. Maybe I had a lot, maybe a few. But you really helped me the best you could. I cannot say I knew you. But we tried.

I am sorry that I always disappeared, but one day I will disappear completely, as we all will. You are precious to me and I love you. I never told you this clearly but it was always true. I can always break this mirror. Maybe I will soon.

THIRTY-SIX

BACK IN THE MIDDLE WITH YOU

He heard knocking on his door. A knocking on his door.
No-one knocked at his door. A knocking on his door.
All he could think of was 'The Raven' by Edgar Allen Poe.
A knocking on his door, Nevermore...Nevermore...
A knocking on his door. Nevermore.
But then he heard Jack.
"Hey Mister, open the door. I know I am the only one who ever visited you. Open the door. It is OK."
He opened the door.
Jack was smiling.
"Hey, Silent One! That was not so hard, was it?"
"Well, as long as you are not beautiful Lenore, it is OK."
"Lenore?"
"Yeah, the girl in the poem, 'The Raven' by Edgar Allen Poe. You know. "Nevermore, Lenore", 'The Raven'".
"You really are a crazy guy these days. Look at this mess. Did you eat some eggs and throw them away recently?"
"Well, I tried to eat some eggs but decided to eat ice instead."
"Oh. That makes sense too!"
"Well, Jack, you have never visited me before. Have you seen any aliens and do you want to talk about it with me? I am all ears."
"No."
"Well, what is this visit about? I thought you liked my monk-alone-in-the-hills fantasy."
"You really are in a rut and are the most non-curious person I ever met."
"How so?"
"Well, what do you think about Mr Kim?
"What should I think? You said he left me a book about Richard Sorge. That was weird. We did not talk about Soviet spies when we were together. That was weird."
"Did you read the book?"
"Yes, the Soviets made a postage-stamp about him, and he had a dedicated girlfriend."

99

"You are incredible. Oblivious is not a good enough word for you. Blind does not do it either. Deaf and dumb does not make it either. Not sure what to say. Infantile is pretty close. Cute but not grown-up also might make it. Did you have a mother?"

"Oh. Yes. I did. I think I had a mother. I almost remember being born."

"Well. Did you ever ask me about my life before you met me?"

"You said you were a priest. Then you were an alcoholic. I supposed the two went together. Besides you were always drunk. I did not expect a good answer from you, or think it was the time to be probing into every detail of your past. I am sorry if you wanted to recite your history. Maybe I should have asked."

"Yes, good point! I was a mess and owe you a lot. But were you ever curious about me and my life?"

"Look Jack, I spend twenty-four hours a day trying to figure myself out. I try to help others sometimes. I am not doing very much of anything. Sorry I did not ask. Is there something you want to tell me?"

"Oh. OK. You have a point. Yes. What I want to tell you is...."

"What, Jack?"

"Not sure what I want to say. Or rather, not sure how I want to say it. You are very hard to pin down."

"Pin down? Just say what is on your mind. You could do that when you were drunk."

"Yes, you are like a mirror. We can see ourselves through you and very clearly. We can never see through you. We just get ourselves back. You never show yourself."

"Sorry. Maybe you are right. What is it? I am a bit surprised by your visit."

"It is just that, well, now you are in the middle of something, and you have not even seen it. – You are the last hope for Korea."

"What?"

"We need your help to save the Korean people. They need our help in the North. We need to do something. This situation has gone on for too long. They need their country back together. They need to be saved from torture and oppression. We need to do something. We cannot have a world or be humans if we let them suffer forever. We cannot forget them. I know you care. Now you can do something. You are the key, strangely enough. You are in the middle of something very big. You just don't know it. You can help save people who are suffering."

"What? How can I do that? Look at me. I am barely hanging on, myself, here."

"Really, talking to you is tiring. I will let Mr Kim tell you. He will contact you soon. Please try to think sometimes. You are a blank. There is a lot going on now. You are the key. But you do not have a clue. And suddenly I don't have the energy to pierce the mirror. Maybe I will come back. Please try to think for once. Try to put the pieces together. Please."

"Oh. OK."

"Look, after I was a priest and before I was the low life alcoholic that you met I was deeply involved in Korea. My wife was Korean and she was killed by the authorities in the North. I really don't like to talk about this or the story. But I loved her very much. Our son is now in his thirties and he never knew his mother. I never could tell him what happened. It made me want to drink. But you stopped that. Now we have a chance to make a difference. Please talk to Mr Kim. He is very important, and he likes you. Please."

"Oh. OK. I will talk to him. I will try to help. Not sure what I can do. You guys seem to know better than me. It's just a bit confusing."

"Yes, life is confusing."

"And eggs taste awful. – Nevermore."

"Oh. I will see myself out. Please try to help. Thanks."

"Oh. 'Nevermore spoke the raven.' – Just joking!"

"I know and thanks again. You are impossible, but we love you."

"Yes. I love you too. Go ahead and go! I hate talking. See you soon, I think. I'll miss you somewhat, I think. Bye, please close the door correctly, if you can."

THIRTY-SEVEN

YOU WERE SOMEONE I KNEW AND LOVED: FOUR

Your dignity was beyond words. You took more from me than anyone should. And you know it. Your position was a mess. You never could conquer my ghosts or the ghosts in the woods. You saw them, you yelled at them. It did no good. There was never going to be any progress in this. How you kept your dignity in the face of them, I will never know. You could never win. It was a fact.

Being decent, clean and dignified did you no good. The blessings of quiet meant nothing to me. I was not looking for the best life or wife. I was not looking for, nor could ever appreciate, the blessings of decency. I loved chaos and war. You were always angry at the sheer ludicrousness of this situation. What were you competing for? The Olympics were over. Phelps was busted for smoking pot. Or not busted as the case may be.

Even if the Virgin Mary or Christ or Mohammed or Buddha or Obama or Reagan or Carter before Iran had appeared in front of us on the road to Kandahar, I would have missed it all. Thank you, Saint Peter.

Tanks on the road to Damascus? No. Or is that a yes?

Sure, I knew it. Sure, I imagined another world. Sure. We should have met before. But Anthony had a wife and was faithful. Cleopatra did not entrance him at all. He was stupid.

It is just revisionist thinking. Lenin did not ride on a German Train to Saint Peterburg's Finland Station and Stalin did not rob banks, and the West is not bankrupt. Something like that.

Oh yes, what route does the opium take out of Afghanistan? Must be UPS or DHL, or is Fedex the best?

What do I say to you?

What do you say to Napoleon on the way back after Moscow? Frozen bodies in the snow, this is a fact. They just found some of them in Lithuania, I think.

Frozen and living in spring.

What do you say after four hours of sex? What do you say to the most deserving woman you have ever known? What do you say when the situation is completely unjust?

When I was always unfair to you, and could never break free; when I was a coward to the truth, what could you say? – "Why?" – Did you wonder what was I thinking?

I would have said, "Poor girl", if it had not been me that you had mistaken. You would have cried, but you had done that already. We are all like moths sometimes. No?

Disaster was your tarot card. You took it. Then you picked it again, and again.

Is disaster a Tarot card?

Ask someone for me, please. But not Gordon Brown, you cannot ask him. Or trust him.

I saw it in a dream. But I never dreamed of you. I should have.

What a mistake!

Princess.

You were the only one who cared about me.

"No. I don't want you to go to Afghanistan. We can live with what we have. It is dangerous there."

I think Lenin's wife was like that. Exactly. – Which wife was that?

I hate Zinoviev and not Kamenev. I don't mean that of course. Or do I?

Litvinov?

Was your dignity beyond me? – Clearly.

Thank you. I should have been with you. – Forever.

Is there no justice in this world? – That should not be a question!

There is no justice in this world. – Yes, it is a statement.

Thank you. You deserve it. You really do.

THIRTY-EIGHT

BLUE CHECKED SHIRTS, SWEAT, AND VIOLINS

Jack left. He closed the door. He did not slam it, but the noise still reverberated in the small room.

He thought about poor Jack.

Jack had been wearing a bright electric-blue checked shirt – maybe it was bright blue and not electric-blue. But is was nice, and went well with his designer jeans and black pointed shoes. He could still see the sweat sliding down the side of his face, and the reddish hue of his forehead, while he was talking to him during this great "call to action".

And he could hear violins.

The question was what sort of violins were they?

We all hear violins at times of high emotion, don't we?

Sometimes they are screeching violins of criticism.

Sometimes they are sweet and melodic, like when we are in love or missing someone.

Sometimes they are jaunty and funny, like when light should be made of a situation.

Sometimes they are the last violins of a dying relative or friend, or a dying child in some nameless, lost valley – sad and mournful.

Sometimes they are pathetic, played by a fool for nothing.

Wow, poor Jack…well…

Jack could be dramatic. And yes, he knew the story already.

Of course Jack could not remember telling him the whole story. Jack could not remember telling him the whole story probably forty times when he was in the alcoholic crying fits of the past. The story was always cute and sad at the same time. But this was his violin tune. Everyone has one, that something so damn meaningful that they think everyone else should just get some of it.

That defining thing; your special violin serenade. You lost your father. You were divorced. You went to Princeton. You were in the military. You are a professor. You love boxing or Aston Villa. You had a great vacation to Kenya. You drive a white Mercedes. Your golf game is impressive. You can cook. You like to read and study military history. You hated your mother. Your business is successful. You cannot get a lucky break. You lived in Los Angeles.

Your family is Irish. You design clothes, or are an engineer. You speak this or that language. You are from this place or that place. You left this country for here and love it more than anything. Your mother died of cancer. Your family was poor or rich. You like to invest in stocks. Your house is worth four hundred thousand dollars. You like to fix engines. You have twenty friends on Facebook. You like Obama, you hate Obama and like Bush. You keep guns at home. You are a great reader. You look great for your age. Your sister passed away. Your brother is successful.

Jack had his violin story and it was sad.

Yes, he knew the story. Jack had been a priest. At some point, he had just lost that special feeling, and left. He then became a patriot and decided to join the CIA. He found himself tracking down and trying to recruit spies. His target for a while was North Korea. He spent several years trying to come into contact with Korean diplomats and Korean exiles in China. He often lamented that, while he was not a great priest, he felt he was an even worse spy. He was falling behind in that job. His managers were unhappy because he never came up with anything. Of course he did not know that it was not easy to recruit North Koreans. In fact it was probably much easier to save someone's soul than to recruit a North Korean spy. Saving souls. How quaint in the valley of broken empires. Or so he thought.

But he did not know that. He had a good heart, and how he went from being a priest to a secret agent was hard to imagine. Really the difference between the two was immense and might be too much to handle and might make you want to start drinking. But that was not the problem at all.

Jack was a good soul and good man and really cared about others. His patriotism was just a natural follow-up to being a priest. He really believed in helping people. It was not a flaw. It was his virtue. A sainthood bonded by passion and the noise of a very broken violin.

But that was not the violin music that was playing in Jack's ears. It was tragedy itself.

It was both tragic and fitting. It was as romantic or disgusting as you wanted it to be.

Really.

Sometimes you want to cry and you just smile.

Sometimes you want to smile and you end up crying.

His one break was his one destruction.

He had met Cho An as a "Korean defector." It was his big break in the spy business. She was working as a bar girl in Heilongjiang Province in Northern China not far from the border with North Korea. Well, she was not really a bar girl, but she was a beauty and a North Korean spy at the same time. That was the story.

It was a good one.

She was trying to recruit him, and poor Jack was trying to recruit her.

So, of course, they ended up falling in love. He said that, in the heat of their passion, he admitted he was a spy. But love had conquered all.

Love.

Love.

Love.

?

?

?

And add another.

?

Jack in his near-violent drinking-bouts would call her a whore and then weep about how much he loved her. She had become pregnant. The child was born. Then she just disappeared.

This was China. He could not go to the authorities; she was an illegal alien, a North Korean refugee.

He was never sure if she was a spy. But Jack later found out that the North Koreans often use bar girls in China as intelligence sources.

But they were in love and had a child. He would argue with himself. She loved me, she loved me not. She used me, she used me not. I was a fool, she was a fool. My life was ruined. My poor son, without a mother.

In any case, his career was over. He did manage to get the child out of China, and did raise him to be a good boy, who never knew his mother. He somehow survived and went into contracting, between evil spells of alcoholism. But this was it.

Kim An became a Mary Magdalene sometimes and the female Judas at others. But, over time, things tend to even out. The female

Judas was slowly exchanged for a martyr. She was kidnapped, he argued, and executed by the North Koreans. That was the story. He was sure.

He could never discover the truth. But, where the stories of our lives are concerned, the truth is always of a very secondary nature, isn't it?

Jack was a good man, with a big heart. You could see that when he cried. You could see that when he tried to be brave. You could see that when he tried to be tough. You could see it as he lived on, aged, and became obsessed with his own story.

Jack would have loved to bite his tongue off, if only he had teeth. Or so he said once at three in the morning, in tears. It was not confusing, given the circumstances, of course. Dental work is important, you could suppose.

Kim An was finally and definitively a martyr. This is what drove him, and nothing else.

But it was OK somehow.

The show must go on, as they say. The wheels go round and round. Row, row, row your boat gently down the stream!

Good advice, isn't it?

And so now, they were calling for the monk to save the day.

Thanks to Jack and Mr Kim, he thought.

He would rather be stoned for adultery than lose his hand for being a thief.

That was obvious.

THIRTY-NINE

YOU WERE SOMEONE I KNEW
AND LOVED FROM AFAR

Maybe you were the German graduate student in Shenzhen that one summer.

Or you were the girl from Chelyabinsk, whom I met at Miami Airport.

Or my great love from Zimbabwe after the trade show.

Or the tall brunette in high school.

Or the Iranian girl I met at university before she went home after the revolution.

You were useless crushes. But I loved you all the same. Thanks, in that case, to the Ayatollah.

Maybe these were just relationships that never would have worked out. But in some ways you were the best relationships I ever had.

Truly.

We never fought because nothing ever happened.

I could think about you, secure that nothing would ever happen.

Yes, I was hurt by you because of something that never happened.

But such a minor crime, it is almost pleasant in retrospect.

And, due to this fact, I could never hurt you.

Your life carried on, so did mine.

Not that I wonder where you are now. I do not.

But you have never left my side.

You were so perfect, because I never knew you.

Not like thirty years of war (and counting until we reach forty more years) over Afghanistan.

Every time I hear a jet overhead, I am in Kabul.

But when I think about you, there are no jets and no war.

When I think about you, I just see you and pleasant defeats, and I wait for more.

I really like to think about the German graduate student in Shenzhen. You were more recent.

I really like to think that I meant nothing to her at all.

And Chelyabinsk with the dark blue eyes, I think of you too.

Or was it Natalya in Uzbekistan? Or Tanya in Serbia before Clinton bombed them?

Some would call all of this a waste of time. Some would say, why waste your time?

Well I am not Einstein. And the flash of their eyes at night or the way they walked was stunning to me.

Such are my sunsets.

Not one regret could I have for remembering and missing them and so much more.

And admit it, we all have the same hearts. I am not the only stupid one.

Thank you. You are always good for a break in this bleak world. You will always be flowers that the spring cannot divide and summer cannot tire, and – to me – that the winter cannot ruin.

FORTY

NAPOLEON IN CAIRO DOES NOT EQUAL CLINTON IN PYONGYANG?

It was obvious. Well, several things were obvious.

Napoleon went to the Grand Mosque in Cairo and Bill Clinton met with Kim Jong Il.

Which was the cultural breakthrough?

Isn't that what we are after?

Don't we want for us all just to get along?

Isn't this an old song now?

Where does David Bowie make his suits?

Freedom and going back home are all relative; unless you have a home, of course.

Better get back to the obvious.

Why do they speak of the silence of the dead?

Why do we equate noise with life and silence with death?

Is it the first scream at birth which condemns us?

Probably.

He thought, enough of this thinking already!

Thinking will just make you think more.

So he just sat there, waiting for Mr Kim.

That was all he could do.

He was not going to read about Richard Sorge or think about someone else's martyred wife.

He was not going to think about the poor souls doing hard labour in North Korea. Why think about them? No-one else does. Better to free two journalists and worry about weapons of mass destruction, than remember sixty years of unbearable cruelty and thousands upon thousands of souls crushed daily.

And yes, they had crossed illegally into North Korea, the poor journalists. – And what about Mr Kim?

Mr Kim was watching the soccer game with everyone else, of course.

What did he care?

That is what it came down to. Did we care?

As humans we could tolerate a great deal, as long as it wasn't happening to us. There will always be cruelty and victims and martyrs. We can just get immunity from the various degrees of suffering and ignore them.

Or can we?

Yes, we can.

Yes, we can.

What is a holocaust after it is over?

What is a holocaust that never ends?

It was like a friend told him once: "Just try not to think about our tragedy all the time. It is our destiny."

Good advice?

So what if the Koreans in the North have been oppressed for sixty years. It is OK as long as they don't attack us.

Berlin Wall...Pyongyang Wall.

Mr Kim.

Mr Kim.

Mr Kim.

Richard Sorge.

Rescued Journalists. Back in Freedom.

Humanitarian Gestures.

Riots at the Auto Plant.

Separated Families and Hard Labour.

One Million Soldiers.

Changes of Power.

Reading Tea-leaves.

It was all insane. As insane as Jack had become, and as we were all becoming.

Or so he thought.

But he should just stop thinking, he thought.

Now they were getting to him. But that was of course after he had been getting to everyone for decades. Such a minor price to pay for such a strong effort.

FORTY-ONE

YOU WERE SOMEONE I NEVER KNEW AND MAYBE LOVED

Hello, Dad.

Yes, you can't hear me any more. My own father. Or maybe you hear me everyday.

Should I just spell it out for the world to see, or read or see, as the case may be.

Dad, I miss you.

Dad, I never knew you.

Dad, I can count our good times on the fingers of one hand.

But it does not matter does it?

I am just like you, some say. But we both knew, we were not exactly alike. I have met many of your friends. You were quite a person. They have good memories of you and don't dwell on your bad points. That is a great epitaph as we wander like ping-pong balls on this earth; usually alone, both of us.

I laugh now when my son gives me a hard time. I laugh, because I know I was worse than him in every way. You had a handful with me, always. I am sure you wondered what you did to deserve me.

You were so intelligent. I am and always will be so proud of the person you were. I am and always will be so proud I am your son.

But, I did not know you. That is a fact. May be now, as I get older, I am finally getting to know you.

It's too late for me now. I will never know all that you knew. But from a purely comparative point of view, I think you would secretly give some praise in your heart for what I do know.

But we never talked about it or this, or anything at all, Dad.

We couldn't talk.

That is just a sad and lonely fact.

And I miss you.

And you left us too soon.

I almost want to cry when I think we could have been friends, if fate hadn't separated us so quickly. It is such a big loss and really took a lot of living away from me.

Tragedy is everywhere.

I know that.

I did go crazy when you left us. Long-term crazy.

I know you loved New York. But since that is where you died. I hate New York and will not enter the place.

Since you died, I refuse to see doctors. I blame them for your death. I won't enter a hospital. My teeth are really a mess now. No doctors since the day you died.

Yes, it hit me hard. Still hurts; the whole thing.

We just need to pick up the pieces the best we can and not cry. So many of us can do that. So can I. Then again, maybe I can't.

You taught me that much, I am sure.

Is it one of the things you taught me, that I was also like my Mother or maybe that I was not?

Is one of the things you taught me that you two did not get along and thus were conflicted by us children?

Or did you separate things like I do?

Damn, I have no-one to ask about this any more.

It is all lost.

I can't get it back.

We can't get it back.

Thank you. I will leave it at that. No, this is not a breakthrough. It is as far as I can go now.

I should do better. I know I have failed again on this one. If I was perfect, there would be nothing to wait for anyway.

FORTY-TWO

NO MORE NOBILITY
DIESEL OIL AND WOODEN TOYS

He should have expected it all.

The young girl was back on the corner. She was again doing nothing; just looking depressed and watching her phone. He did not bother with her. He did not speak to her. He knew what she was doing, and he had finally figured it out when he passed her one day and she was speaking Korean into her phone.

He continued with his routine. The girl would come and go. No-one paid him any attention at all. Or so he thought. Well, he knew better of course. Besides the girl regularly on the corner, there suddenly appeared two young Asian men in a black Corolla sitting on the road in front of his place. They would come and go, and so would the young girl.

It was so over-dramatic. It was so useless. He continued to ignore the silly game. Why does everything need to be so damn important and interesting? Love, war, hate, success, and ambition are so damn dramatic. We gloat like fools. We act mysteriously for no reason.

The girl and the two guys were watching him and for no reason. He never went anywhere and never did anything. What took so long to find out? Really it was over-dramatic. Like fools in a play, like actors playing the violin; again they were doing nothing but acting like fools. He knew the game and the foreplay was doing nothing. It was all for nothing.

Then the next night, when he was staring at the wall like any sane man should, he heard a knocking at the door. It was, of course, Edgar.

"Hi, Edgar, let me guess why you are here! You are a friend of the young girl outside my window."

Edgar looked a bit shocked. "What young girl?"

"Look outside! That one!"

"I....Well maybe she is another of your girlfriends. What do I know? You do tend to break hearts, from what I hear."

"Ha, ha. Well the list is long, yes. But look at her; not really my type. Not exotic at all. Look, Edgar, don't lie. You know her. Let's not go into this ridiculous fantasy any more."

"Well..."

"Yes, don't lie. It is just not you. It is the Mr Kim-Mr Hussaini-Jack-and-Edgar Club in action. Or is it a cult thing?"

"No, we are not a cult."

"What a relief, Edgar! What a relief to my soul and the wasted moments of my life. You guys are acting more stupidly than your enemies. I am not surprised you lose every battle."

"Yes, we lose; but we have not lost the war."

"You mean, therefore, that there is something to win in this life?"

"Compassion is a victory."

"Yes, I will remember to ask the Maitreya Buddha about that next time I see him on the subway."

"Well, he might like the subway; it is the gate to the underworld."

"And I guess sending people to watch me all the time is good policy; so compassionate. You know I am just sitting here like a sane person, watching the wall all the time. You know it."

"Well, you were not too kind to Jack the other day."

"Not kind? Are you sure? Were you there? I have known you guys for years. Are you selling diesel oil and wooden toys now?"

"Diesel oil and wooden toys?

"Well they do go together, at least to me. Think about it next time we are not together. OK? And this whole thing is just ludicrous!"

"Well, we want you to help."

"Well, Edgar, I really want to help myself."

"You would be a great Inquisitor."

"Yes, you are right. But I prefer to torture myself. It is more fun. You guys would all make terrible torture victims. Don't cry any more, Edgar. Just let's get this stupidity over with. You all make terrible mystery persons. Why don't you all just go to Jerusalem, or Mecca or Gujarat or the Cape of Good Hope or something? Watch the Ashes or the Roses or go to that god-damn awful golf-course in Scotland. You all deserve a low score like Tiger Woods. That is the secret in golf, no? Get on with it. I am going on a Gandhi-esque fast until you fools get your act together. Did you hear me? A Gandhi-esque fast and I am fasting not for the liberty of India but in prayer for diesel oil and wooden toys! OK? I said I would help. But you are so boring. Just know that! To quote Pink Floyd, Edgar – and I will sing this –

> And did they get you to trade your heroes for ghosts? ...
> Hot air for a cool breeze? Cold comfort for change?
> And did you exchange a walk on part in the war, for a lead role in a cage?

"Or Edgar –

> So, so you think you can tell Heaven from Hell,
> blue skies from pain.
> Can you tell a green field from a cold steel rail?"

Edgar looked stunned.

"OK, Gandhi! Just wait. We will be back. You are crazier than you think."

"Fine, Edgar. I will be fasting in utter non-noble boredom. Just for you and all souls, and for diesel oil and wooden toys. The Maitreya Buddha knows I am right. And Edgar, you know it too."

He frowned. He left. He slammed the door, just like Jack had done before. Or was that his mother? Or, to quote Pink Floyd again:

> How I wish, how I wish you were here.
> We're just two lost souls living in a fish bowl, year after year,
> Running over the same old ground.
> What have we found? The same old fears.
> How I wish you were here.

And the poor girl was still standing looking at her cell-phone, with the two guys in the car outside on the street, just like before.

FORTY-THREE

YOU WERE MY MOTHER – ONE OF THEM

What do you say to someone who saved your life? What do you say to someone who made you a functional human? I would not have made it at all without you. I would have been in gaol. I am just that stupid. Without you I would not have had a life.

We did get along fine when we were together. We did not get along fine a lot of the time. I would say now,. looking back over forty years, well I did not get along with a lot of people. It would be easy to blame you, or easier to blame me, or easier yet to blame someone else. But in the end, I will just blame myself.

I am not sure really who to blame.

You did a great job. You took a disaster and made it run. If I got anything done it was because you were willing to go toe to toe with me every day. It was no easier for you than for anyone else. I guess I cannot blame you for anything. I guess at one point your circuits were just fried by my behavior. You probably wrote me off like almost everyone else has. I was impossible for you and so many others. Really, I have decided that no-one should have to be with me every day. It is just too much for anyone.

So I understand. I was too much. You were right.

In the end, I really don't think you liked me. – Love? – We never got there.

But you knew I loved you.

That much I achieved. They always know when I love them. Equally everyone knows when I do not love them. I am very clear. I always was. Sorry you had to inherit this legacy. Instead of saying thank you, I should be saying, I am sorry.

I am not sure you had a happy life. I think you were not sure either. But you had the life you had. It had lots of good moments and I was lucky enough to see them. You were great. I probably never said that to you. That was a big mistake. I am sorry.

In some ways, or in more ways than I want to admit, I am worse than I want to imagine. I should have told you. I played the angles and just said what my selfish self would allow.

I always have the "I am confused" excuse, don't I?

117

In your case, I did just enough and because of that I did not do enough. Just enough is not good enough with those we love. It never is. I know that now. Pathetic.

I owe you so much. Just enough?

I am bitter. I am bitter at you, but much more bitter at myself.

I want to eat cardboard when I think of this.

I want to eat glass, because I made you eat it so many times.

Thank you. I love you. You worked so hard for all of us. I never responded. I am a stupid mule a lot of the time. You knew that mule only too well. Mule or fool? Does it make a difference?

FORTY-FOUR

WILL WE EVER GET TO THE PLACE WHERE WE HAVE NEVER BEEN? FASTING FOR NOTHING: DAY ONE

Well, that was all that he could think of.

"Will we ever get to the place where we have never been?" Call it the Twilight Zone. Call it Nirvana. Call it Happiness. Call it Peace on Earth. Call it the Great Beyond.

Well, if you call it death, it does not sound so good. If you call it Paradise, that sounds better. Will we ever get there? – Faith! It just stands up and then flops down like a drunk. – Faith! You call it and then what?

Philosophy and Metaphysics aside, and the Nature of Mankind and Womankind aside, what are we doing here, really?

Such was the nature of fasting, even stupid fasting with no reason. He just was not going to eat. The big question when you fast is, can you drink water? Or can you drink sugared water? What about ice? Is that allowed? Thinking useless thoughts is most definitely permitted.

It is what you do, when you are starving yourself on purpose. You ask yourself deep soul-searching questions and wonder what you can eat. This of course, has benefits. Since you are doing this on purpose, well it was your choice. But what do people who are really starving, without a choice, get to think?

Yes, it was not a noble fast. Yes, it meant nothing and yes it was ridiculous. But that is just how he was. He would do stupid, stubborn things. He would get crucified in public, and beg them to do it. He would.

Yes, the black Corolla was still there with the same bored-looking young men. Yes, he was starving.

Thanks, Edgar. Thanks, Jack. Thanks, Mr Kim. Thanks, Richard Sorge.

How did he get into this silly situation? – Save Korea? Sure, save Korea! Made sense. What were they thinking? What did he have to do with Korea? Who were these guys? Let us not forget the statue in the rain. In fact he was not bothering anyone. Not really eating. It was as if he was not even there. He was not really bothering anyone. Why all this? Was it some sort of mass delusion? Could he burn a witch? Was a Nobel Prize in his future for this? Wow, such a pinnacle to a useless life; or was it the precipice to a greater fall?

He had done everything he ever could to stay away from people and now he was the key to world peace! He was laughing. They were not. Weird was not the word to describe this. Absurd? – Yes, that sounded better. Bizarre? – Not right. They were clowns in a monster movie. – That was it! – But then again, we are all clowns in monster movies these days. That is what it was all becoming, anyway. But just keep the rest of their clowns away from our clowns, please!

They were picking the wrong guy. He could not wait to find out what their evil, incompetent design was. There were so many idealists. – Use them!

He was just a cynical – in his own little world – part-time writer, who was poor and probably a poor writer at that. – Oh the horrible irony! – Bring on the clowns, bring on the aliens! There was a way out.

What way out? – He hardly went outside. His special prison was all that he had left, and he liked it. Now they were coming for him. It could be classic paranoia but there were two guys outside his building who sometimes followed him. It would be a bad dream if he ever slept. He did not want even to think about it.

And then he thought about Angela. He did not know why. Forget her for the moment and my – what was it? – Obliviousness? – He hoped that was not a word in the English language.

"Yes, Angela. Thanks! I am oblivious to everything."

He said that aloud. Was talking to yourself a crime? What about thinking to yourself? That must be OK. We all do that. We all think. We do not react. We are not conditioned to react or think the way we do. No. That was impossible. We are logical, competent beings. Everything in our lives made total sense. – He completed that thought with the silent words, "To yourself". It made him laugh aloud. – Is it possible to laugh in silence? – He had seen that look before. They are looking at you and they are laughing, and you can't hear it. He then composed a short hai ku poem for the occasion. Not really.

Eyes that smile, and mouths that blink.

Clowns in Horror Movies that make you creep.
Mr Kim is keeping me from my sleep.
Why Oh Why?
And.... I don't like to speak or think!

Creepy Clowns.

Will we ever get to the place that we want to go?

Oh! Not that again.

He looked through the small peep-hole of his door. Was anyone outside? Maybe Mr Kim was about to knock on the door. Yes, he could do that. Spend the whole day looking out of his door. You can look out, but they cannot look in. He thought that was how it worked. That must be the secret of the universe.

What happened to the "let's just wait and let it happen" guy of the past? Where had he gone?

And yes, you can drink water when you are on a useless stupid fast.

He ate more ice and was thankful for something.

FORTY-FIVE

DAY TWO OF THE FAST FOR NOTHING
SOMETHING UNIVERSAL: SOMETHING GALACTIC

At some point it hit him.

There was something going on. No. It was not Mr Kim or Jack's wife. It was beyond them. There was a disturbance in the universe. Something was going on. It was not about the Earth; it was bigger than that. And other entities were just as confused. It was coming from far away. Even the three kings were looking for it. Maybe he was one of them.

Anyway it was calling to him and it had just happened. Surely they were trying to make contact with him. They were watching him. Not Mr Kim. Or maybe…?

It had just happened. The water was falling, but not landing. Things were sliding up and sideways and around and not down. He could feel it. Things were not right. He probed his third eye. Yes. Not right.

He wandered into the city night, trying to detect something. The same child was riding her red bike in circles. But she was wearing pink boots. The guy with the white jump suit was wearing sunglasses in the night. He searched high and low.

He saw a building with light blue windows at a distance and another building with tall sharp spires. He saw a guy with grey hair in the middle of his head and all black at the sides. He saw a woman wearing a black plastic bag and that was all. He saw some police cadets in white and black, marching in the dark. He saw a son who looked just like his mother. He was searching for something that would confirm his feelings. Surely everyone or someone or anyone had felt the same thing?

The natural thing would be for all of them to be out searching. When you can hear screaming in the universe, or something has broken, everyone turns around. It does not need to be a plate in a restaurant or a car crash on the highway or the screaming candy-red of the fire-engines as they pace the night.

He knew that the tectonic plates that were holding everything together had slipped, cracked or been forced. It was beyond all of them and beyond everyone on the planet. He looked at the people's feet, he looked at their eyes. He saw them breathe. He watched them exchange money. He saw racks of meat and men carrying jugs of water. He watched the girls in love talking on their cell-phones. Some people saw him. Others missed him. But he was looking at them all for a sign. Were they looking at him for a sign?

He put on his sun-glasses in the night. And no-one noticed. They were UV. He could see with them. Shouldn't there be a laser show? Or maybe the situation was so far away and so complicated, so intergalactic that no-one could feel it yet.

There should be a grouping. He could not be the only one so disturbed by the arrival of such far and such undetermined news. Maybe they all felt it. He would keep checking and look for signs. There should be something.

A call from Angela! "Hey, where are you? Have you been eating?"

"No, Angela. I am fasting for nothing. Are you OK?"

"Not really. If you have time, come over to see me!"

"Oh. OK. Oh. OK. Where?"

"Well our love-nest would be fine. I can't stand your place."

"Well, great. I guess that is part of the galactic question."

"What?"

"Nothing. I will be there sooner, as opposed to later."

"OK. That I can understand. Bye."

He looked around to see if the Asians were watching him. No. They were long gone. He guessed they only worked when he was at home and they were therefore not working. Perfect. He did not want to get Angela tangled up in all of this. Or maybe she was one of them. She never called him. He always called her. Must be something wrong, or maybe he had performed well last time. Never could be sure with her. Oblivious. That was funny.

He had to figure it out. But how to get to the love-nest?

Yes, it was his and Angela's place. A little room on a small street without traffic. She paid for it. He had a key. He could use it only if he wanted to write there and did not leave any trash or eggs or mess. So he never used it. At least Angela loved him for his writing. She really did. Whether she thought him oblivious or not, she loved him for something. Maybe he wasn't that involved in the day-to-day of her emotions. But she loved each and every thing he wrote and was there to cheer him on.

It was nice to have somewhere to go – the first time in a while. Though he was slightly upset to leave his quest for the upset in the universe, he decided to keep looking on his walk to the nest. It was a hard decision to make. What if those he was searching for were right around the corner and Angela had just messed up something really big for him?

He stopped in the street. Turned around. Turned back around and proceeded toward where Angela was waiting for him. – Oblivious? – That was funny.

Walking on their small street without traffic, he saw the light was on. She was there. He saw some children playing football in the street. He realized they were smart little things. This was the only street without traffic on it in the whole city. They sure knew where to play. – Oblivious? – That was so funny.

As he climbed the curved, wooden stairs, he thought he was going to let her have it about the oblivious thing. But when he entered the unlocked door, he saw the small black stone table with two candles burning and two bottles of wine. Angela was in the glow of the two flames, and she was crying.

"Angela? Are you OK?"

"No. I just had a big fight with Freddy."

Freddy was her husband of twelve years. He had been with her before and after the wedding. Freddy was the other man, whom he could never bring himself to ask Angela about.

"You never fight with him. What is going on? What happened?"

"I think he has a lover at the office."

"Well you have a lover, Angela. Well, it is true. We hate when people do things to us that we do to them."

"Yes, but you don't count. You are my life, beyond a lover."

"Thanks. I will take a few years to figure that one out, if you don't mind."

"No, it's just – I don't know – I needed to be with you. Please listen to me, darling."

"Well, I am all ears, obliviously." He just had to get that in.

Angela laughed through the tears. "You are a jerk. I really do need you."

"Thanks."

"With Freddy – well, you know! We are happy like stones on a mountain. Unmoving."

"Like that Japanese movie, *Kagemusha?*"

"Yes...." She laughed again.

"Well, Angela, you know the story of that one. Never leave the mountain. Hold your position. Keep the rival warlords at bay. Never come down, and hold the ancestral lands."

"Yes, well I think Freddy has moved his banners to the North. He has been going to Beijing a lot and talking to some tall Northern bitch."

"Northern bitch?"

"I think she is from Dalian. I heard him planning a trip with her on his phone from the bathroom."

"Wow. Sorry."

"I know I have a double standard. But I do not count you. You are the love of my life. You were always there. And nothing more. You never bothered me. I could never bother you. Freddy, well that was different. He has always bothered me."

"Well, shall we have some wine and forget about this?"

"OK, I will try." She drank the whole glass in one gulp.

She drank another and another, and another. And then another. They finished the first bottle in fifteen minutes.

"Angela, that is enough. You have to drive home."

"Not tonight... What were you saying about something galactic?"

"I think the universe has a struggle going on now, one that we have never seen as humans."

"What? Is that what you think of all day long?"

"No, I felt it some hours ago. I was sure. It was beyond all of us. It was happening in a very far-off realm. The Earth has nothing to do with it, but some of us here are affected. Maybe you. Maybe you, tonight. It is disrupting everything and every plan, thought, action and love-affair, as well as every conversation and thought. It is as though all was suddenly changed for all of us, and nothing can be the same again. I was out looking for signs when you called me."

"Some hours ago? What time?"

"I think it was something like 10pm. I think I had been sleeping. Some time before I thought about you."

"That is when I fought with Freddy."

125

"Yes, something is going on. The hearts and minds on this planet are beating strangely. It is not a samba or drums or violins, it is a new and disturbing music and no-one and nothing has heard it before. Nor am I sure whether it is a friend or foe. But I have been called to help. So I went out to see what was there."

"Did you find anything?"

"Not yet."

She held his hand. "Maybe it is a new dawn for all of us. You know I love you."

"I hope so and you should. I mean, what would your life be without me anyway? A new era would be good. The last era was desolate and segregated, especially for us."

She held his hand and came over to embrace him. She fell asleep in his arms, drunkenly. He carried her over to the bed. He had always enjoyed sex in the morning more anyway. And this would be fun. He always liked those drunken take-off-your-clothes bouts. They were the best.

He finished the bottle and fell asleep at her side. They woke up naked and smiled. Angela had great teeth and flashed them as she said, "Another great job my dear. I feel wonderful; like a new person. Thank you."

"Well, good! – And thank the galactic struggle!"

"I will. Have a good day! I am off. I will call soon."

She showered and cleaned up, since he never would; and with that, she was gone. She always left like that. It was always the same experience.

Short, sweet, devastating, memorable – and yes, just what he needed. And tragically sad, at the same time.

Thank you, Mr Kim.

Thank you, creepy clowns.

FORTY-SIX

THE FAST: DAY THREE

Well, at least he got a good sleep for once. He put on his clothes. He did not even shower. What was so dirty about sex anyway? He always felt some love for Angela, even if they were never really together, and yes, she was right that he hardly thought about her at all. But yes, it was love, just not the way anyone wanted it to be. But maybe that was changing too.

On the way back to the eggs and the ice, he was still looking for some sign that things were changing. He knew they were. Where were they? Someone would talk to him about this.

When he got back home the Asians were back and not looking very happy. He had lost them and they were unhappy about it all. Good for them. He silently wished them a nice day in the car, and watched the sun hit its zenith with satisfaction. Black conducts heat. They would be cooking all day. He really preferred the statue. He should not have blown her cover with Edgar. That was stupid. Besides she was kind of cute, a little fat but kind of cute. The two Asian guys were just plain boring.

Funny, he felt better.

Nothing like a little human warmth to change your attitude.

He was glad he had talked to her. He was glad she felt she needed to talk to him. He should really thank her for being there for so many years. She kept him from his own madness and even listened to some of it. And thankfully the word oblivious was not heard or seen in the early dawn. How was it for you Angela? He did not need to ask.

He ate twelve ice cubes and felt full.

It was alright. The stars were changing. Angela loved him. Mr Kim and gang absolutely adored him. He was not alone. He could look outside through the peep-hole in his door and wait for the knock that would come. He just hoped he would not starve to death before then, as he was feeling a bit faint. But wine is nutritious, isn't it? Sure it is.

Issue number one on the agenda was still the universe. What had happened?

He knew who had been calling him. It was the aliens he had seen as a child. Jack and Edgar had seen them also. Recently his children had been having incidents. But his kids were smarter than him and could chase them away when they came. As for him, they were leaving him alone. Maybe he knew too much now. But they were calling him just the same. They were disturbed, so he was disturbed. They needed him, so they called him.

Mr Kim?

Well, who knew? He was pretty strange. Koreans do like to dance. So did they. But they dance to communicate. Why do we dance? Does it take an earthquake to wake us up, or do we just need to dance? What would that do to the universe? I wonder if they are dancing disco in Moscow. He had heard that somewhere. But yes, we are dancing twenty-four hours a day. Kali and Ganesha make sure of that. The few remaining sufis do too. Are we moving the Earth out of its orbit or global-warming it?

What are we doing and will we ever get to the place we have never been? What are we doing and will we ever get to the place that we have never been?

It was back. He tried to shake it but the questions kept coming on. Same questions, same tone. Same questions, same tone. The fast was making him insane in its own useless way.

FORTY-SEVEN

THE FAST: DAY FOUR

The elation of the aliens and the universe was ending. He was starving. He was sad. He became even sadder when he remembered the day a long, long time ago when Angela had told him she was getting married.

It was a lovely winter day. They had just gone to eat at – where else? – an Indian Restaurant. Angela looked at him and held his hand.

"How would you feel, if I told you I was getting married?"

"I would laugh first. Then cry later."

"But you will always have me. I am really in love with you."

"Then why would you get married, Angela?"

The conversation was getting very strange. It was one of those conversations that you never really want to have. The whole idea of losing her to another man was becoming more and more disturbing.

"Well, you know how you are. With you I could never have a family or a real life. You are too unpredictable and never could live with someone every day. I want a family. I want a life and a home. With you there would be none of that. Not to mention you are really not a one-woman man. You're just that way. But I do love you … and forever."

It was becoming beyond disturbing. It was turning into a crushing blow. She was an angel, a bright intelligent sweet angel. She had done everything she could to gain his affection. She was wonderful beyond words. The world was ending. He felt he could be losing her. He wanted to cry out from the stranglehold that was crushing his heart deep inside his chest. He almost could not speak.

"I know you are just joking, right?"

"No, Darling, I am not. I am engaged and we will have our wedding next month."

"I can't believe, Angela, you did this to me. How could you get engaged and not tell me. I mean, how?"

The tears were beginning to fall. They were his tears. He was destroyed and he knew it was too late.

"Angela, no. You can't!" That was all he could say between the tears and what was transforming from tears into sobs.

"Don't cry," Angela said softly. "You will make me feel terrible about this."

"Then feel terrible. I just, just cannot believe you are doing this to us."

"But I am not. I always want to be with you. I love you."

"How could you love me and get married? What are you doing to me?"

"Please just try to understand. It is too late to change it now. I am sorry."

Between muffled gasps and tears falling, he got out one more comment. "Yes, sure, Angela. Later you will know you made a huge mistake. You can't get married just like that. You can't even love him. You love me. Later you will know. This is a tragedy, Angela, for you, for me. I just can't believe it."

"Yes, maybe you are right. But, I will always have you. You are mine and I am yours."

He was not sure if that was compliment, a put-down, or a life sentence. It somehow made great bloody sense, all of it. She was talking of eternal love and would be saying her vows to another man, next month. He really wanted to die before the calendar could change.

It made such great and wonderful sense, didn't it? Yes, she was making a mistake. He knew it. But like all disasters, and even those with an end in sight, it just made it worse, knowing there was no way to avoid it and knowing that his heart was broken asunder.

With that she got up and left.

It was the beginning of a new life. He cried all night.

Part of him knew she was right. It was true. He could not live with anyone for long. He could not provide a life for anyone. He would never be a great father or there for birthdays. He liked to eat alone. He liked to stay up all night writing. He had no money and no prospects. Why would a sweet angel like Angela stay with him? He could give her nothing more than a deep and solid love, sometimes. He could not bear the thought of her being with another man. He knew he had lost everything. He knew it was another of his greatest mistakes. – Another of his greatest mistakes! – With him, they were all greatest mistakes, not great mistakes. They were all the greatest. He had lost her.

In his mind he could see her having his children, and raising them with care. He could see the birthday parties and the thought of the wedding tore his heart out. What had he done? He had lost her. The fact that she said she loved him was not a salve for his pain. How could she do that? How could someone be so pathetically practical? That was all she was doing. She was just being practical. She was making sense. She could see beyond the passion and soft embraces and jokes told at three in the morning. She was making a life for herself. There was none to be had with him.

Pathetically and tragically practical.

And it was all his fault.

He even knew the story before it started. She would learn to hate her chosen, practical life. She would come back to find him. She would cry and say she was sorry, but by then it would be too late to end her marriage because of the children. She had destroyed two people that day.

He had to live, knowing that it was he who had ruined her. She had to live, believing she had ruined herself. It was a tragedy and there was no way out. They were both sentenced to sure and certain sadness. Their lives were ruined that day.

He was angry with her for not realizing this. She could never figure things out very well or see the into the dim distance. He was disgusted with himself, because he was – well – because he was who he was. And because he was who he was, the angel had left him for misery. He could hardly bear the thought, and tears came whenever the thought rose up from his chest.

He snapped out of the memory and went back to his fast, useless though it was. He did not want to think about that tragic disaster again.

But he went right back to it with the pain growing again in his heart.

After that day he did not see her for about eight months. He could not stand the pain of seeing her and was tormented hourly by the thought of her wedding and honeymoon and the first months of wedded bliss. He was just waiting to see how long it would be until the dam broke open and she was back with him. Those were the longest eight months of his life and the saddest.

Then it was just as he knew it would be. She came back to him. She cried. She said it was her fault and her mistake. They were together again and then she went home to her husband.

He could not bear to ask even once in all these years about the other man, the beneficiary or victim of his mistaken and eccentric life. Freddy.

The other man, who had the perfect wife, who did not love him. Freddy.

The other man was probably suffering also. Freddy.

And so the tragedy went on; through the birth of her two beautiful children, through the vacations and cruises, events and parties. The gaol sentence continued on, for them all, cruel and definite. The maze was without an end. It was the perfect trap.

He wanted to hate her. He knew he loved her.

As time went on she would make funny comments. For example:

"You were right. This life of money does not equal happiness."

"I should just have stayed with you. No matter what happened, you always treated me well."

"My life is empty. You were right. You were all I ever had."

He always wanted to scream at her when she said things like this. Yes. It would have been so different. They would have stayed married. He would never have got divorced. They could have started a brave young life together. She had cut it all. Their hearts were wounded now and it was hard to accept that she was responsible for all of this. She was wrong. He had been too young and stupid to stop her. He had not done enough and now they were both lost.

Yes, he still loved her. He had to. She had nothing else and he had never wanted anything else. She stupidly had killed them both so long ago. What a tragedy; it was funny. The worst part was, there was nothing to be done about it. He just had to accept, there was nothing else to do.

Sweet tragedy.

He laughed for the first time that day.

"Oblivious, Angela? I am oblivious?"

That was funny.

He felt everything, including the growling of an empty stomach, and an unsteady walk as he reached for more ice and thought about eggs uselessly. And he did not cry, but rather cursed Mr Kim and this stupid fast that was turning out to be for nothing. Oblivious? Tell that to the galactic situation, if you dare.

FORTY-EIGHT

RANDOM ACTS: YOU MAKE MY DAY

You called to wish me a happy birthday. You said I was looking better and better. You smiled at me for no reason. You treated me like babies treat each other, smiling and kind, before we learn to hate. You called me "sweetheart" or told me "I love you" and it meant everything. You don't even know how good it felt.

How many birthdays have I forgotten? How many smiles have I not given? Anniversaries of this and that, I cannot remember anymore. Did I even ask about you? Did I laugh when you fell? Did I wish you well? Did I realize you were struggling through this life also?

I probably did not. Pushing myself meant more than you. I liked the separation of walls and closing of doors. I loved it. I loved my separation. I loved my quiet. I loved myself more than I loved you. It was so much better to be alone than to be with you. I figured it out finally. I figured wrong.

Even when I was kind, I imagine many of you were treating it like a respite before the next blow fell from heaven. I could be so cruel. I made you immune. My sweetness and my evil were about the same to you in the end. You called me brilliant. But I was just brilliant at keeping my distance from you. What a total waste! A million missed opportunities. I did as I was taught. I did it so well.

I marvel myself at the distance I have created from everyone and everything. I marvel at how I got exactly what I wanted. I marvel that I wait for the final separation more than I wait for the final reunion. I hold my mountain. You could not climb there if you tried. Everest is nothing compared to my hill and separation.

Thank you for the birthday wish. Thank you for the smile. I am sure you did it just as a reflex. The sweet child I was has only become a mountain god. A great mountain god obscured by clouds, not worth your time trying to understand anymore.

FORTY-NINE

THE FAST: DAY FIVE
MR KIM – BREAKFAST FOR FREDDY

He knew by the fifth day he was stupid. But there is honour in stupid stubbornness. He was proud that he could hold out against Nothing. He was proud that he could push the wind. It was one of his greatest calling cards. It defined him, this great stupidity. He was feeling both starved and stupid at the same time.

Time for more ice.

Yes, it was stupid. He was fasting for nothing. No-one cared at all. Mr Kim and the aliens were not paying even a bit of notice.

Edgar and Jack. What a joke!

Angela and Freddy.

The LeBarres.

The Korean girl and the Asian guys.

The work he was not doing.

The stupidity of his stupidity.

It took just five days for him to notice. That was funny. Yes, maybe he was oblivious.

No. Not a chance. He was just stupid. And not always, just on this fast thing. It is important to support yourself sometimes. You might be right and not know it. There is always that chance.

He stuck out the fast for a few more hours, finally realizing that it made no difference.

For the first time in a week he decided to go outside. What would he see that he had never seen? Well the first thing he saw was new. The building across the street was green and blue. He had never seen that before. There were clothes hanging out from the second floor. The lights above the door were still on.

What more would he see?

He walked his usual route to the restaurant. The Korean girl was missing. The Asian guys were gone. See? No-one cared at all. No-one was after him. The few people he saw were looking ahead of themselves and paid him no mind. No reason to be suspicious at all. In fact no-one noticed him and he noticed all of them.

Of course, when he got to the restaurant, he was mortified to see Mr Kim sitting at his usual table. He was looking at a photograph of Richard Sorge.

"Well, hello, Mr Kim. Surprised to see you."

"Yes I have been waiting for you. You must be very hungry. Edgar said you were fasting."

"Oh, you know Edgar? Funny you did not mention that in Seoul the last time!"

"Yes, I know Jack too. And Mr Husseini."

"So what is going on with you, Mr Kim? Jack said you needed to save Korea."

"Well, yes. We need your help."

"Who is we?"

"We are a lot of people and no-one at all. We are just trying to do what is right."

"Well, everyone thinks like that in some way, I imagine."

"Yes. Maybe."

"So what is this about? I can't dance very well at all. You said all South Koreans wanted to do is dance."

"Yes, it is true and it is sad. What a funny reaction to the screams of thousands so near to them."

"Screams?"

"Yes, the screams of the million in the torture camps and labour prisons."

"What is your story, Mr Kim?"

"Do you care? Jack said you could be oblivious at times."

"Oblivious?"

"Well you never ask anyone about themselves. You don't seem to care, as if you had figured it all out before."

"Is that oblivious or arrogant?"

"Maybe a bit of both. You are tough."

"My heart is bled dry, Mr Kim, as I am sure your heart is also."

"I am not sure I ever had a heart; especially after I sent my own mother to the camps."

"I am sorry to hear that. Yes that would be quite a burden. But remember we all send everyone to different camps when we ignore them or don't care."

"Interesting. I never saw it that way."

"Well, try it sometime. You were never married, I guess."

"No. How did you know?"

"I did not know. But thanks for the book on Richard Sorge. I did read it. Quite a person, indeed!"

"Glad you read it. What do you think about him?"

"Well – excitement and story apart – I wish he could have seen the postage-stamp. Quite impressive! I did mean to ask, after all this time, do you like living in the South, where you can hear the screams of the torture victims so close?"

"No I don't. I can hear the screams and I see them dancing. I have been made sad by all of this."

"Yes, funny how we cannot hear the screams. May be our own screaming inside drowns them out?"

"Yes, or our own selfishness and separation. But you can help us change that."

"Who is us, again? – If you don't mind my asking."

"Well, Jack and Edgar are some of us. We want to stop the screams."

"So, who is at fault?"

"We all are. As you said, the Americans, the Chinese, the Russians, the Japanese and yes, the Koreans on both sides."

"Why the South Koreans?"

"They are just as bad. They live on, knowing what is going on. They dance and fumble around, play sides and produce LCD TV sets in China. The suffering is never the main issue. They just try to cope with a terminal disease."

"Do they have a choice?"

"We all do. That is certain. To allow this crazy situation – as you said – go on for sixty years is without reason, without humanity and without sense. We are not humans any more. We drink Coca Cola like monkeys. We get married and die for nothing. How can we live with ourselves?"

"Good question. I agree. Not sure about myself either, any more."

"Jack and Edgar know your heart. It is good. You helped them. That is why I am here to ask you to help all of us. You are very important."

"How can I help? Please do tell me."

"Well, you know Angela, your lover?"

"What does Angela have to do with this? How do you even know?"

"We know a lot. Yes, you are both very careful. The Indian restaurant is the key."

"You have been following me?"

"Yes, for a long time. Jack and Edgar know."

"Wow! Thanks! It does get me mad. My relationship with Angela has nothing to do with you."

"Well, Jack was an intelligence officer."

"Yes, and he was a priest."

"Yes. Once again you don't understand. Jack was both an intelligence agent and a double-spy for the Vatican at one time. The relationship with the Korean girl hurt him badly. He really wanted to help convert the Chinese to Christianity. But he was ruined in every way."

"Yes. – So he was a double-spy, like Dear Richard Sorge."

"Yes,.."

"And Edgar is a spy for the King of Thailand?"

"Yes and no. He was also a spy. But you already know what brought him down."

"Yes, the affair with the young man made him leave the Monastery."

"Funny, you know a lot. But you do not know everything."

"Well, Mr Kim, do give me time. I am getting there, minute by minute."

"Yes, you are."

"So what is the thing with Angela? What does she have to with Korea? She has never even been there."

"Do you know anything about Angela?"

"I did once, but I have not cared for a long time. It is a long story."

"Do you know where she works?"

"Yes, she works for a rich woman in one of the banks."

"Do you know what Freddy does?"

"Freddy. Freddy. Freddy. – Now you are going to make me cry. No. I do not know what he does, and never asked."

"Well, this is about Freddy in the end."

"Why?"

"Who was the one who ruined Jack by setting him up with the North Korean spy? Who ruined Edgar by introducing him to the young man?"

"Not a clue! – Freddy?"

"Yes, Freddy is in charge of Chinese Intelligence here in the city. He was in charge of the North Korean spy effort in the North of China before."

"He was? How do you know?"

"We know a lot. We need to. We are sick of the screams."

"And what can I do about this?"

"Mr Kim handed him two DVDs."

"This is what you can do."

"What is this?"

"It is everything. It has the war plans for all countries in case there is a new Korean War. The American plans, the Japanese plans, the Russian plans, and those of both Koreas."

"Oh."

"It has a list of all the prisoners being held in North Korea and where. There is also a list of those murdered in the past thirty years. And detailed maps of each camp."

"All here?"

"The DVD also has a list of all those involved in these crimes and others, including Americans, South Koreans and Chinese. It is a compendium of all those who have committed crimes against all of us and should be charged with crimes against humanity. And yes, the poor souls in North Korea deserve to be defended, like all of us. If you say no to mass murder, you must say no to the mass murder of Koreans too."

"Quite true, Mr Kim! But Americans? What have they done?"

"Yes, there are those who have been corrupt. And Japanese and Chinese who have profited from working with the North, or from not caring at all. It is quite a list."

"Yes, sounds like it."

"What do you want me to do?"

"Well, every morning Angela and Freddy drive to work together. He listens to music and leaves his wallet in the left-hand glove-compartment of his car. I want you to put a DVD in the middle of his wallet. The one with his picture on the back."

He looked at the DVDs. One had a picture of an Asian man in a military uniform.

"This is Freddy? I never saw him."

"Yes, that is your Angela's Freddy. I would have thought you would be glad to get back at him."

"No, not at all. Get back at him for what? My heart has no blood any more. Remember?"

"Oh, very well! I understand, but I really do not need to. I wish my problems were as minor as yours. But we do appreciate your help."

"What will Freddy do with this?"

"Not sure, but we are giving out about a hundred throughout the world to different people. Each DVD has a list of who is receiving it. So Freddy and all his colleagues will know. For those not implicated, the guilty ones are in for a surprise like never before. We are going to end the screams."

"Why?"

"Everyone is implicated. So if one of them destroys it, there is always someone else who will know what they have done. The evil ones are all in this together. We are all in this together now. There can be no cover up of innocent death anymore."

"What has Freddy done?"

"He has gained, through Macau, millions of dollars for helping the North Koreans ship goods and arms through China, and he has also worked against the Americans and Japanese."

"Some of that would make sense. He is a Chinese military officer, it seems."

"Yes, true. But his comrades will not like his illegal activities."

"So, if I was Freddy, I would just destroy this."

"Well, he can't. Others will see it and it has valuable information which he must pass along."

"If he doesn't?"

"Then he is finished. He might as well just run away. But this is serious."

"What about everyone else?"

"This DVD will change the world. They cannot fight because their plans are laid out in minute detail. They cannot escape because their crimes are listed. They will all need to think about what they are really doing. Much of this will be published in the press and on the internet in a matter of days. We need your help now. You are a key piece in all of this. I guess you never thought you could be so important?"

"But what about the North Koreans? How are you going to pass this over to them? It can't be an easy thing to do. And what can they do?"

"Yes, this is a very hard part. But they know that later they can be called to account for their terrible crimes. Maybe this will make them think. They definitely cannot start a new war now. Everything is laid bare. They would be defeated. We have all their plans. Several dozens have already been murdered for trying to help us compile this information. There may be more deaths coming, but finally the screams will end. It is time."

"So you have people on the inside in all of these countries?"

"We do. Believe it or not, there are still good people in all those countries. You might be surprised. We can change the world. The screams can stop. We still have a conscience. For every corrupt soulless person, there is another who knows this world can be better. For everyone with hate in their hearts, there is another with the heart of a child and the courage of lions, willing to make a difference. We just cannot see them in the open any more. In this world the good need to hide behind the evil ones and not the other way around. But that too can change. For every cynic, there is still a dreamer. Life can and does mean something. We can right the wrongs. Some of us are not crazy and cruel. We know you are one of us, even if you do seem oblivious to so much."

"Thank you, Mr Kim, for the kind words! So this is a secret organization of good people?"

He thought he saw a yellow light from Mr Kim's eyes.

"Yes, it is. Now you are one of us. There is something going on."

"Oh, the universe is changing. I had a dream or notion of that."

"You could say that. Yes, you could say that. I am sure you will help us."

"How do I get this DVD into Freddy's car?"

"You can it figure out, I am sure. I know you will succeed. Korea depends on you. The future of the world depends on you."

"Now you sound like Jack! – Do you have an alcohol problem?"

"No."

He laughed with yellow eyes.

"I have the same problem as you do. I need to make up for my mistakes, and now."

With that he stood up, bowed and left. He forgot his picture of Richard Sorge.

When the waiter came over, he ordered eggs and water with lots of ice. He could finally eat. Funny, though, he was suddenly not hungry.

FIFTY

YOU WERE LIFE ITSELF. A FINAL THANK YOU

I finally figured it out. There is nothing to understand. None of us understand any more than the next one. There is nothing to figure out. You and I are equally confused. For this I am relieved. It was not just me. For you I am worried. You were my best shot at sanity. But, no. We are all in the same boat.

Thank you…it is all so clear now.

TO BE CONTINUED

THERE ARE OTHER STORIES TO BE WRITTEN.

FIND OUT MORE ABOUT PROVERSE AUTHORS, TITLES, EVENTS AND LITERARY PRIZES

Visit our website: http://www.proversepublishing.com

Visit our distributor's website: <www.chineseupress.com>

Follow us on Twitter
Follow news and conversation: twitter.com/Proversebooks>
OR
Copy and paste the following to your browser window and follow
the instructions: https://twitter.com/#!/ProverseBooks

"Like" us on www.facebook.com/ProversePress

Request our free E-Newsletter
Send your request to info@proversepublishing.com.

Availability
Most titles are available in Hong Kong and world-wide
from our Hong Kong based Distributor,
The Chinese University of Hong Kong Press, The Chinese
University of Hong Kong,
Shatin, NT, Hong Kong SAR, China.
Email: cup-bus@cuhk.edu.hk
Website: <www.chineseupress.com>.

All titles are available from Proverse Hong Kong,
http://www.proversepublishing.com
and the Proverse Hong Kong UK-based Distributor.

Ebooks
Many of our titles are available also as Ebooks